Contents

DATES,

dOUBLE dATES

and BiG, BiG

TROUBLE

KAREN McCOMBIE

SCHOLASTIC

for alice MiLLeR (aged 83½)

-the PRincess of alexandRa PaLace

Scholastic Children's Books,
Commonwealth House, 1–19 New Oxford Street,
London WC1A 1NU, UK
A division of Scholastic Ltd
London ~ New York ~ Toronto ~ Sydney ~ Auckland
Mexico City ~ New Delhi ~ Hong Kong

First published in the UK by Scholastic Ltd, 2001

Copyright © Karen McCombie, 2001
Cover illustration copyright © Spike Gerrell, 2001

ISBN 0 439 99869 7

Typeset by TW Typesetting, Midsomer Norton, Somerset
Printed by Cox & Wyman Ltd, Reading, Berks.

10 9 8 7 6 5 4 3 2 1

The right of Karen McCombie to be identified as the author
of this work has been asserted by her in accordance with the
Copyright, Designs and Patents Act, 1988.

PROLOGUE

Dear Mum,

I came across that photo of you and Dad the other day – you know, the one from your first date. The one where you look a bit weird, 'cause you've just thrown up...

Anyhow, it just reminded me how much I loved it when you used to tell me about how you two got together; all the stuff about how he'd come into the jeans shop in Camden High Street where you worked and try on loads of different pairs every week, just to have an excuse to talk to you. (He never bought any, did he?)

And better than that was how *you* used to spend your lunch-hours in the bike shop he worked in across the street, buying a bell one day, a bicycle pump the next, even a puncture-repair kit.

Then, when he finally *did* ask you out, it wasn't till that first date that he found out you didn't even *have* a bike.

It was so sweet the way you told Dad that you didn't mind about him getting the cinemas mixed up that first night out together, and taking you to see a horror movie by accident. *Even though* horror movies and the sight of blood usually made you feel ill. And it was *really* sweet of Dad to still fancy you after you threw up on his lap.

True love.

After all that, I guess I wouldn't have been in the mood to hand someone my camera like you did and get them to take a photo of the two of you (I think if it was me, I'd have wanted to forget the whole thing, after puking all over the place). But I'm glad you *did* decide to do it – or we wouldn't have had a record of the time our parents started seeing each other. I don't know if you had a proper kiss that first night (I hope not, under the circumstances), but it's still one of the most romantic stories I've ever heard – even if there weren't exactly string orchestras playing in the background and rose petals raining from the sky.

Hope it happens to me like that one day (but maybe minus the part about being sick).

Not so long ago, I thought it might ... and that was also right around the time when me and Linn and Rowan started to realize that Dad had found someone to replace you.

I suppose you'd better hear this from the beginning...
Love you lots,
Ally
(your Love Child No. 3)

Chapter 1

THAT FIRST KISS (I WISH...)

OK, so when it comes to the whole romance thing, I admit, I daydream about it a lot. And I mean a *lot*.

I daydream about it when I'm walking the dogs up by Alexandra Palace, looking out over the sprawl of London off in the distance. I daydream about it in bed at night, when I lie in the dark and stare out at the stars through the tiny skylight in the roof of my attic bedroom...

So that sounds very poetic and everything. But then, I *also* daydream about all things romantic at distinctly *un*romantic moments. Like during especially boring classes, or when I'm brushing my teeth, or when it's my turn to do the laundry and I'm sorting through my family's dirty socks, or even when I'm helping my little brother Tor clean rabbit poo out of the hutches in the back garden.

I don't think Juliet thought about Romeo when she was cleaning out rabbit poo. Well, when I think about the film, I certainly don't remember seeing

Claire Danes in a pair of yellow Marigolds day-dreaming about Leo DiCaprio shinning up to her balcony while she was trying to shoo away an irate bunny who's in the mood to bite.

Maybe the fact that I can daydream about romance at really inappropriate times means I'm very imaginative. Or maybe it means I'm a weirdo – I'm not too sure. But anyway, one of my favourite daydreams is That First Kiss. It goes like this...

1) I go to a party and, magically, I look like Joey out of *Dawson's Creek*. (Look, it's *my* daydream, so stuff like that can happen, OK?)

2) The party is amazing, the music's brilliant, and most brilliant of all – I spot *him* across the crowded room. (The *him* part is interchangeable, depending on who I've got a crush on that week. I fall in and out of fancying different boys pretty regularly – but having said that, there's only one boy that I've stayed constantly and truly mad about, and that's my sister Linn's mate, Alfie. Sigh...)

3) During the evening, there's lots of tantalizing staring and looking away going on between us, just to get a bit of a *frisson* going. (Good word, *frisson*, isn't it? Except I said it to my best friend Sandie once, and she thought it was some kind of fish. But I tell you, having a bit of a fish between you *definitely* isn't romantic...)

4) The lights are low and sparkly, my favourite track comes on (that changes week to week, daydream to daydream), and from nowhere *he* sidles up beside me and asks me to dance.

5) Right, this is where it gets good... I've got my arms around his neck, and I can feel myself shiver with goosebumps as he pulls me closer to him, his hands on my back. We say nothing, just look into each other's eyes – reading each other's thoughts and knowing instinctively what's going to happen next. In slow motion, we move towards each other, tilting our heads gently as the moment gets closer. I can feel the warmth of his lips even before they touch mine. And then...

I was sitting on the usual bench on Ally Pally, letting my First Kiss daydream drift through my mind, and was just about to melt mouths with Alfie, when the mood was suddenly ruined.

Well, it's inevitable really, when you find yourself in a headlock.

"Billy! Get off me, you total moron!" I yelled, trying to tug his arm away from around my neck.

Out of the corner of my eyes I could see a middle-aged couple walking along the path looking kind of concerned. They probably thought I was being attacked by some lunatic, and who could blame them? They weren't to know that it was just my mate, acting like a complete prat…

They weren't the only ones looking concerned; my two dogs – Rolf and Winslet – didn't know who to bark at first: Billy, or his yappy little mutt Precious, who was already up to his usual tricks, trying to inspect both their bottoms at close quarters.

"Do you give up?" I heard Billy asking, though I couldn't see him since he was standing behind me and the bench.

He must have been watching that stupid wrestling programme again, I sighed to myself.

"And are you going to give up acting like a six year old?" I managed to growl. "God, no wonder you can never get a girlfriend…"

It was a low blow (Billy's mighty sensitive about his lack of success with the girlies), but still he didn't let go.

It was time to get tough.

I reached back and, after a couple of searching slaps, found his nose and pulled it hard.

"Arghhhhhh!" he whined, letting go of my neck and scrambling over the back of the wooden seat, with me still hanging on to his nose.

The couple walked past at that point, staring disapprovingly at us – a pair of delinquent thirteen year olds spoiling the serenity of their Saturday-morning stroll. They obviously didn't approve of the barking dogs either, eyeing up Precious, Rolf and Winslet like they were the spawn of the devil. (Course, that might be true in Precious's case.)

"Gum on, Ally. Led go," pleaded Billy, nasally. He sounded like he could be in an ad for Night Nurse or something.

But you could tell he was quite enjoying it, since he was now sitting beside me with his hands on his thighs, making no attempt to make me stop.

"You look ridiculous," I told him, as I gave his nose an extra tweak for luck.

"You'll look more ridigulous in a segond when I blow snot all over your hand..."

"You wouldn't dare..." I said, narrowing my eyes at him.

"Wouldn'd I?" he grinned.

He took a big breath, ready for blast-off, when I let go and jumped off the seat.

Rolf and Winslet thought this was a cue for playtime, and bounded over to me, tails flapping about enthusiastically.

"Billy – you are the most disgusting boy I know!" I yelled at him.

He grinned again, put his hand over his nose and made the most grotesque snotty noise.

"And you *laaaaaaaave* it!" he roared, getting up

and running straight towards me, holding his hand out like he was going to rub it in my face.

I was pretty sure he'd just blown a raspberry behind his hand, but I wasn't taking any chances, not where snot was concerned. So I did the only sensible thing – I ran.

I wondered what the couple were thinking now, seeing a screeching girl, hurtling down the hill pursued by three mental dogs and a deranged boy in a baseball cap. They were probably thinking that they were glad we weren't *their* kids…

"Gotcha!"

The red gravel path that led to one of the park entrances was just hurtling into view when Billy grabbed me by the waist and rugby-tackled me to the grass.

"Get off!" I yelped for the second time so far, feeling him land heavily on top of me.

"Aha! You will never get away from the evil Hand of Snot!"

Somehow I managed to twist around underneath him, grab the evil Hand of Snot with both my fists and force it *well* away from my face.

"Billy – grow up!" I panted in his face, trying to sound angry – and trying just as hard not to laugh.

"Ooh! Listen to Ally Love! She's *so* sensible!"

teased Billy, putting on a dopey voice. "Well, we'll have to do something about *that*..."

With his free hand, Billy started mercilessly tickling me, running his irritating fingers from my waist to my armpit to my neck and back down again.

"*GERRROFFFF!*" I squealed breathlessly, between giggles, but he didn't – not that he'd have been able to hear me above the din of three barking dogs anyway, all of whom thought this was an excellent game.

But somehow, I heard another sound above the racket.

They say mothers can tune in to the noise of a crying baby, no matter how faint it is, or even if it's not their own baby. Well, I managed to tune in to a crunch of gravel on the nearby path, and the rubbery screech of bike brakes (when your dad runs a bicycle shop, I guess it's in your blood). Of course what caught my attention most was my name.

"Hi, Ally..."

As I turned to look at the source of the voice, I tried to brush Winslet away with one hand, but she carried on happily licking my face, regardless. I didn't realize it at the time, but I had my other hand right over Billy's face.

"Whas-going-on?" Billy mumbled, trying to shake his face free of my splayed fingers.

But I didn't answer him – I was too busy staring at the vision in front of me, perched on his mountain bike.

"Hello, Alfie…" I smiled stupidly, waggling my dog-licked hand at him in a half-hearted attempt at a wave.

Talk about bad timing.

I had why-don't-you-just-kill-me-now-before-I-die-of-embarrassment timing…

Chapter 2

LINN IS WAY, WAY, *WAY* OFF THE MARK

It's funny how you know when you're being stared at.

"What?" I demanded, catching Linn gawping at me for the seventeenth time in the last hour or so.

We were in the living room – me (on the sofa), Linn (next to me on the sofa), Rowan (on one of the armchairs painting her nails silver) and Tor (on the floor, driving his toy cars over a mountain range played by snoozing Rolf) – aimlessly watching a rubbish quiz show after stuffing our faces, this Saturday teatime.

I'd seen Linn eyeing me up earlier over the kitchen table, studying my face like I'd grown another nose or something. And ever since we'd come through and flopped in the living room, she'd kept up the surreptitious scrutiny, even though she was supposed to be flicking through the work section of the local paper in search of a Saturday job. And here she was, at it again...

"What? I'm not doing anything!" said Linn,

opening her green eyes wide and looking shocked at my accusation. "I'm just reading this!"

"Well, if you're trying to read it, then here's a handy hint: keep your eyes on the paper instead of on *me*," I said, sarcastically. "Anyway, who's going to give *you* a Saturday job?"

To tell the truth, I didn't mean to be so mean. And anyone in their right mind would give Linn a Saturday job; she's pretty, well-presented and polite. (Polite to other people, that is. Not to her sisters...) It was just that I'd got myself in a bad mood ever since Alfie had caught me in a compromising position that morning. And it was all Billy's grandad's fault. Well, what I mean is, if his parents hadn't planned to visit Billy's grandad on Sunday, I could have met up with Billy as usual – instead of swapping to Saturday – and Alfie wouldn't have seen me like that: i.e. lying on the grass with Billy sprawled across me like a wet blanket, and a dribble of dog drool dangling off my face, courtesy of Winslet.

"No need to get snippy with me, just because *you're* in a bad mood..." said Linn, in an infuriatingly righteous voice.

My big sister Linn is an expert in being infuriatingly righteous. In fact, I might be wrong, but I think she's doing it as an A-level...

"I'm *not* in a bad mood!" I said, sinking further into my bad mood.

"Mmmm…" muttered Linn dismissively, flicking noisily through the pages of the paper.

"I'm *not*!" I protested.

"Whatever you say…" shrugged Linn.

See what I mean? It makes me so angry when she goes all big-sister-superior on me like that. It makes me want to … I don't know – ruffle her immaculate hair or go and mess up her colour-coordinated knicker drawer, or something else that would ruffle her perfectly organized feathers.

"Shut up, you two! I can't hear what he's saying!" Rowan snapped at us.

It's not that my in-between sister (in-between me and Linn, age-wise) was particularly wild about corny Saturday-evening game shows; it's just that she's kind of super-sensitive and hates bickering. Even though she and Linn bicker on a practically daily basis.

But, hey – we both shut up. Linn glued her eyes to the newspaper and I stared blankly at the TV screen.

"…*and now, name an animal indigenous to Australia!*" said the cheesy, toothy TV presenter.

"A marsupial!" Tor piped up, not even glancing up from his game.

Rolf snuffled and flicked his tail as a fire engine drove over his furry haunches.

"That's too smart, Tor!" muttered Rowan, fixing the top back on her nail varnish with extended fingers. "All the contestants on this show are picked to be thick, I reckon. They wouldn't be able to *spell* marsupial."

"*Come on, Keith – an Australian animal! You can do it!*" the presenter encouraged, a despairing glint in his eye.

"Duck-billed platypus!" said Tor, as the participant on the screen chewed his lip and struggled to come up with an answer.

"*Still* too smart, Tor," I chipped in, trying to take my mind off Linn and her snide remarks. "All they're looking for is 'kangaroo' or 'koala', and that bloke will win a car. And he can't even get that!"

"*Barrrrpppp!*"

The buzzer meant the bloke on the screen was out of time. Bang went *his* chances of winning some fancy four-wheeled drive.

"*Well, time's up I'm afraid, Keith. Didn't you even have a guess there?*"

"*Um,*" muttered the bumbling bloke on the telly, "*I thought maybe … a sheep.*"

Me, Rowan and Tor burst out laughing –

especially Tor, who saw ignorance about animals as a sign of deep human failing.

But I stopped laughing pretty quickly – as soon as I felt Linn's eyes on me once again...

"What!? What is it?" I demanded to know, swirling my head around quick enough to catch her squinting at my neck.

"Ally, is that a *love* bite?"

"*What?*" I frowned at her.

She'd *got* to be joking. With my track record of pitifully few romantic encounters, there wasn't much chance of me getting *that* lucky.

"There!" she said, extending one finger out to touch me on the side of my neck.

"Get off!" I said, echoing my words to Billy from earlier on in the day.

I leapt up off the sofa and hurried over to the mirror by the living-room door. The mirror was almost a piece of art in itself; Mum made it years ago. She'd bought a plain mirror-tile for a few pence, Dad told us, and then added the whole frame of Fimo flowers and elves that swirled and peeped at you as you stared at your own reflection.

I hauled down the neck of my jumper and tried to see what Linn had seen. Sure enough, there was a dark shadow; but on closer inspection, it was easy to see what I already knew – that it *wasn't* a bruise.

"It's mud! That's all!" I exclaimed, licking my finger and rubbing at the smudge of Ally Pally dirt, still in place after Billy's rugby-tackle earlier in the day.

"Dirt?" said Linn, raising her eyebrows at me. "Well, that's not what Alfie said…"

"What do you mean?!"

"Well, Alfie said that from where *he* was standing this morning, it looked like Billy was snogging you on the grass up on Ally Pally…"

I opened my mouth and shut it again. What could I say to Linn that would put that thought right out of her head, without admitting that the only boy I'd happily let snog me was Alfie?

"What? You and *Billy*!" said Rowan in surprise.

Great – now Linn had *her* believing it!

"It wasn't like that!" I yelped to both of them. "We were just mucking about! We *weren't* snogging!"

"Uh-huh," murmured Linn, disbelievingly.

Arrrgh! She was off again…

"Look," I said, struggling to explain myself. "It's ridiculous. It would be like you snogging Chazza, Ro; or you, Linn – it would be like you snogging Alfie!"

Urgh. The very thought…

"Me and Alfie? As if!" snickered Linn. "Anyway,

stop trying to hide it. If you and Billy have got something going on, then…"

But I'd stopped listening: my radar ears had now tuned into what was going on out in the hall.

It wasn't the fact that my dad was talking on the phone; it was the fact that he sounded like he was *whispering* on the phone.

"What is it?" asked Rowan, spotting straight away that I wasn't paying a blind bit of attention to Linn's wind-up any more.

"Shhhh!" I muttered, with one ear to the living room door.

The door thunked as Linn and Rowan darted over and barged into me, wanting to hear what I could hear. Even Tor slunk up silently, ducking under our arms and placing his ear at pole position at the tiny gap in the door.

"Yes, it was great, just like old times…" we heard our dad say, sheepishly.

Linn stared hard at me, and over my shoulder at Rowan, who was standing behind me, her hot, anxious breath on my neck.

"It's been a long time, that's for sure…"

"What's going on?" Rowan whispered. "What's he on about?"

Shhh! mimed Linn, with a finger

"…yes – definitely. I would love that…" my dad

muttered. And then, with a small, wry laugh, "No, I haven't told them yet…"

Linn fixed her eyes on me, her stare saying exactly what I was thinking. I couldn't see Rowan's expression, but I felt her trembly hand on my shoulder.

"You don't think…?" I whispered.

"Shhh!" said Linn, dropping her gaze downwards to the top of Tor's head.

That was the problem. We'd always protected Tor from stuff, and we couldn't let him know that we were all thinking the same thing.

Was this… Could this be something to do with *Mum*?

CHAPTER 3

THE TALE OF THE INVISIBLE MUM...

"Ally? It's me – can I come in?" Linn called out softly from the other side of the door.

I'd become very popular all of a sudden. Normally, around eleven o'clock on Saturday night, I'd be the only one in my room (the odd cat included, and *all* our cats are odd), unless Sandie was staying over, which she sometimes did.

But tonight, my room was like a magnet; three (out of five) cats, both dogs and my sister Rowan were taking up space inside my four small walls and under my slanted roof. The cats – Frankie, Colin and Fluffy – were already here when me and Rolf padded upstairs after a non-eventful night in front of the telly with Dad and Tor (my social calendar wasn't exactly packed this particular Saturday night). And Winslet had followed Rowan in when she'd come tapping at my door (Winslet – smart but grumpy dog that she is – obviously sniffing out that this was the place to be).

At this rate, I was expecting to open the door

and see Mad Max the hamster leading a procession of iguanas, white mice and stick insects up the stairs from Tor's room at any second.

"Yeah – come on in!" I replied, keeping my voice low.

I didn't really want to alert my dozing dad that there was a bit of a family pow-wow happening upstairs in the attic.

Linn had only opened the door a crack when a cat that wasn't Colin slithered his black and white body through the gap. He scampered past me and Rowan, who were sprawled on the floor, and leapt – light as a furry feather – up on to my bed. At closer range, I checked out the fight-chewed ears and sussed out it was Eddie. All we needed was for cross-eyed Derek to come scratching at the door and we'd have a full house in the feline department.

"Oh..." said Linn, looking a little put out to see that Rowan had beaten her to it.

"Hey, Linn – how did it go tonight?" I asked our eldest sister. "You're back early, considering you were going to a party."

"I left early – I wasn't in the mood," she shrugged, shutting the door behind her and joining us on the floor. "I kept thinking about Dad..."

I couldn't blame her; I'd spent the whole evening pretending to watch whatever was flickering on the

J 301098

TV screen, when all that was really running through my head was Dad and that weird phone call.

(Still, imagine being at a party with Alfie and choosing to leave! But then Linn doesn't see Alfie the way *I* do. That girl's *got* to need specs – it's the *only* explanation. Specs, or a brain transplant. One of the two...)

"Me too," said Rowan, running her hands through her dark curls and sending her Indian bangles jangling. "I was round at Chazza's tonight, and he was showing me and Von what he could play on his new guitar—"

Linn rolled her eyes at the thought of how boring *that* sounded, but thankfully, Rowan was too distracted by Frankie padding on to her lap to notice.

"—but I couldn't stop thinking about Dad," Rowan continued. "And what he was saying on the phone and ... everything."

Everything ... meaning Mum. Or at least our suspicions that his conversation had been to do with her.

Or even *with* her.

"So, Ally – did he say anything about it tonight?" asked Linn, leaning back on her elbows on my threadbare carpet, then sitting up again smartish when she felt how uncomfortable that was going to be. "Anything at all?"

"No," I shook my head. "He just made jokes about what was on the telly, then went up and read Tor a bedtime story. The usual."

Me and my sisters hadn't had the time or the opportunity to talk before Linn and Rowan had gone out. For one thing, Tor was there (and we didn't want to set his little mind whirling), and for another thing, Dad came blustering in to the room as soon as he'd finished the call, cheerily demanding to know what rubbish questions he'd missed on the quiz show.

(You should have seen how fast the four of us moved when we heard the phone go *ping*! as he put the receiver down. One second we were behind the living-room door – the next we were all back in our places on the sofa etc., trying *very* hard not to sound out of breath.)

"But once Tor went to bed," Linn continued to quiz me, "didn't he even give you a little hint then?"

"No, he didn't say anything. No hints, nothing."

I'd just been through all this with Rowan, and I knew what Linn's next question was going to be, mainly 'cause Rowan had asked it thirty seconds before Linn came knocking.

"Couldn't you have pumped him for a bit of information?" asked Linn, right on cue.

"No. I thought about it, but I couldn't work out what to say that didn't let on that we'd been listening in on his conversation," I tried to explain.

But it was no good – my two sisters were looking at me with total disappointment. I'd been their only hope to solve the riddle this evening and I'd failed miserably.

"So, do you think he *could* have been talking to Mum?" asked Rowan, finally saying out loud what we'd all wondered.

I'd thought of nothing else for the entire evening, but to be honest, I couldn't see how it could be true. I couldn't believe that Dad would keep anything to do with Mum a secret from us (except for Tor – we *all* kept things secret from Tor, for his own sake). Especially not after four whole years...

So maybe it's a good time to tell you what happened with Mum. It's more complicated than you might think, mainly because there're are *two* versions: the short one and the long one (otherwise known as the white-lie version and the truth). I might as well tell you both, since the first one doesn't take up much room...

Tale of the Disappearing Mum (the short version): this is the one Tor believes. Mum loved all of us so much that she felt terrible about all the children in the world that have no one to care for them. That's why she decided to go away for a while – leaving us in Dad's safe care – and work for a charity that sends her to faraway places. There are lots of countries out there and lots of children to look after, and that's why she's been away so long. But she'll be home one day...

Tale of the Disappearing Mum (the truth): basically, Mum was only seventeen (and Dad was twenty-two) when the two of them started going out. Mum had just finished school and was working in the jeans shop in Camden, but was planning on hiring a craft stall in the market to sell all her paintings and pottery, then using the money she'd make from that to take off round the world for a year, before going on to art school. That was the plan. Then – oops! – she found out she was pregnant with Linnhe (think: Linny. Not that any-one calls her that. Except Rowan, that is).

Anyway, once they'd got over the shock, Mum and Dad were blissfully happy; and, by the time Mum was eighteen, she found herself in her own little flat, married to Dad and with a small bundle of baby to look after.

Fast-forward through ten very happy years (and they *were* happy – I remember lots of it, even though some of it's kind of hazy now), to the time when Mum had Tor. All of us knew that Mum had changed a little bit; she still laughed and had fun with us, but we'd sometimes catch her looking sad, even though she'd say she was all right ("Post-natal depression that just didn't get better," Grandma explained to us much, much later). Then, when Tor was three, Mum and Dad had this long chat with us girls one night (Linn was thirteen, Rowan was eleven and I was nine), and announced that Mum had decided to go travelling for three months, to see some of the places she'd meant to visit on that long ago year-round trip she'd had to cancel. It didn't sound too long to us; we were big girls and could cope, helping Dad around the house. It would be an adventure for us too.

Next thing, she'd been gone six months – always sending cheery letters and postcards home to us – and we three girls began to get suspicious. We *definitely* got suspicious when Dad started to get gloomy and Grandma sold her house and moved to a flat just along the road "so she could look after us better". I don't know when it was exactly that we all began to think she *wasn't* coming back, but eventually that's the way we all saw it, and the way we've expected it to be ever since…

(But you can see why we stick to the first version for Tor. You don't want a little kid to think he's the one to blame for his mother disappearing off into the sunset, for ever. It would be pretty tough to handle, figuring your Mum got ill 'cause she brought you into the world. The nice, fluffy, charity-work story is a lot better for him, if you see what I mean.)

So here we were now – the three eldest of the Love children – wondering if we'd got it wrong; if Mum really was closer at hand than we'd thought.

"Well, all that 'it's just like old times' and 'no I haven't told them yet' stuff Dad was saying on the phone," mused Linn. "It definitely *sounds* like he was talking to her."

"And he did go out on Wednesday night," Rowan chipped in, her face all taut and tense. "Remember? He said he was going for a drink with the guy from the plumber's next door to the shop."

"Oh, yeah…" I muttered, remembering Dad hastily scrambling out of the door, looking slightly overdressed just to go and sink a couple of pints in a local pub.

And we were bound to notice when Dad went out; he did it so rarely. After Mum left, I think he felt he had to over-compensate for the fact that we were one parent down, and he always tried to be around for us.

"And he'd done his hair that funny way – all

greased back. Like it was in some of those old photos of him and Mum when they were young. We were teasing him about it," Linn reminded us.

"Wow, do you think the pub story was just a cover?" asked Rowan, wide-eyed.

Frankie was trying to wriggle out from her heavy-handed stroking, I noticed.

"Maybe," shrugged Linn. "Maybe he got all dressed up to go and meet *Mum* somewhere..."

"But, hold on," I said, scrambling to my feet and going over to the big map of the world on my wall. "We got a letter from Mum last week, and she was *here*..."

I pointed to a blue pin stuck on a small island in the Pacific Ocean. Every time we get a letter from her, I check where it's from and mark it on my map.

"So?" said Rowan. "What difference does that make?"

I can be a prize-winning worrier, but Rowan *really* gets herself in a stressed-out mess. You know, forgets to engage her brain, she's so busy panicking. And right now it wasn't just the look on her face that was giving her away; it was the fact that she had Frankie in a vice-like grip in her arms. Poor Frankie – he'd only been looking for a warm lap to sit in and he'd found himself being used as a feline worry-bead.

"*Think* about it, Ro," I urged her. "Mum wrote that she was planning to stay where she was for a couple of weeks, so—"

"—so she *couldn't* be back yet," Linn finished off my train of thought.

"Probably not," I replied, not sure whether to be reassured or hideously disappointed by that realization.

"So, if it wasn't *Mum* that Dad was talking to on the phone," Rowan said slowly, "where does that leave us?"

"Back at square one," I sighed, flopping down so hard on the bed that Eddie – much to his surprise – found himself bouncing off the duvet and up into the air.

SANDIE'S SMART THINKING

Q: What's white and red, and drips all over?
A: My mate Sandie.

Well, that would be the answer, this one particular Sunday afternoon.

Sandie's face had gone waxy white, but her rotten cold had left her with a scabby red nose and upper lip as a fashionable contrast. Add to that two nostrils that were running like taps, and you get the picture. (And it wasn't pretty...)

"How are you feeling?" I asked.

Stupid, really, since it was so obvious how she was feeling. And that was *lousy*.

I noticed that the carpet beside her bed was strewn with soggy, scrunched-up paper hankies, even though there was a wicker wastepaper basket strategically placed within chucking distance. But not placed strategically enough, by the looks of it.

"I feel absoludely derrible..." sniffed Sandie, punctuating her medical update with a parping blow into a man-sized tissue.

Her big Disney eyes were particularly pathetic –
all dewy-wet and sad. Or maybe she looked more
like one of the bunnies out of *Watership Down*.
Maybe the one with myxomatosis…

"You don't *seem* very well," I agreed, which was
an understatement.

I was perched on the end of her bed, well out of
the catchment range of tissue-chucking.

"Id's really sweed of you to come – bud you
shouldn'd have," she scolded me with a grateful
smile. "You mide cadge this cold!"

"Great! I get a legitimate excuse to stay off
school!" I joked.

I didn't mean it. It wasn't like I loved school to
pieces or anything, but I'd much rather have been
going to classes than looking as bad as Sandie did
right there and then.

I moved further back on the bed, and hoped I
was well out of the germ radius.

Maybe it would have been a better idea to just
phone rather than visit.

"So, I guess *you* won't be coming back to school
tomorrow…" I said, astutely. Not.

Sandie shook her head. She was like this
disembodied head (a white, red and dripping head)
above a sea of cutesy teddies. Cutesy teddy duvet
cover, cutesy teddy pillowcase, matching cutesy

teddy pyjamas. All bought by her mother, I hasten to add. No fellow thirteen-year-old friend of *mine* would willingly sleep amongst cutesy teddies if he or she had freedom of choice...

"Mum says I'll have to sday in bed a couple of days ad leased," she mumbled forlornly, through her bunged-up nose.

I couldn't blame her for sounding down. Sandie's mother was one of those suffocating, over-protective mums at the best of times. But if Sandie was ill, she'd be even worse – fluttering about, plumping up pillows and shovelling her daughter full of medicine every five seconds.

The thing is, much as they love her, Sandie's parents are the reason she comes round to my place so much. They're both about a hundred and ten (OK, so I exaggerate, but her folks *are* old), and treat Sandie (their only kid) like she's a cross between a china Dresden doll and a precious, delicate butterfly. Thank goodness they approve of me, or Sandie would have no fun at all. Mind you, they've never seen my house. They would probably never let her through the door ever again if they saw how ramshackle our place is (despite my Grandma's best efforts to civilize it). And if they knew how many animals there were, they'd be apoplectic about Sandie catching cat-flea allergies, or distemper from the dogs or something.

"Ally, can you do me a favour?" Sandie sniffed, pointing over to the candy-pink painted table by her bedroom door.

Honestly, you should see her room. Everything in it is pink; and not that mad, raspberry pink that Rowan's done her room in (which sears your eyeballs to the back of your brain, but is still somehow cool). No, everything in Sandie's room is in shades of candy or bubblegum pink. With frills. It's like being in Life-Sized Barbie's room, for God's sake.

And Sandie hates it.

I know, I know, it was her choice in the first place ... but that was when she was *eight*. She's been desperate to redecorate it for the last three or four years, but her parents won't let her. They think her room is "just adorable". If you ask me (and even if you *don't* ask me, I'm going to tell you), I think it's 'cause they want to keep their little girl *little*, if you see what I mean. Growing up, having periods, snogging boys; I think they've blocked all that out and are just pretending it's *never* going to happen.

(And, just for the record, Sandie *is* growing up – she's got bigger boobs than me, but then *every*one does; she *has* started her periods – aged twelve at my house and Linn sorted her out; and she *has* kissed boys – even though it was just during games of Spin the Bottle and that kind of stupid party stuff.)

"What is it? What are you after?" I asked, scanning the top of the table, and hoping Sandie didn't seriously want the white teddy sitting on it with the silk heart that had "We wuv you!" embroidered on it. (A Christmas present from her parents. *No*, not when she was at primary school; *this* year...)

"Can you pass me thad new box of dissues off the dable?" she asked.

I had to laugh.

"You sound just like Billy did yesterday," I smiled at my own joke.

"Whad – does he have a cold doo?" frowned Sandie, all concerned.

"No," I shrugged. "I was just torturing him by twisting his nose off."

"Why?" Sandie quizzed me, looking confused.

"He's a boy, he's annoying ... what more is there to say?" I shrugged.

It's funny; Billy's my oldest mate and Sandie's my best mate, but they just don't really hit it off together. They like each other and everything, but they just don't seem to gel. We do all go out as a threesome sometimes – mostly to the movies, where they don't have to speak to each other too much – but usually I see them separately. Billy's told me he thinks Sandie's too quiet, and he doesn't know what to say to her. But to be fair to Sandie, he *does* tend to act more stupid and show-offy in front of her. Nerves, I suppose. And Sandie says she thinks he doesn't like her, which to me translates as Sandie feeling a bit insecure about me having another close friend, other than her.

It gets on my wick a bit, actually, but I like both of them so much that I don't let it bother me most of the time.

"So whad did you do lassed nide?" asked Sandie, using her nail to spear the new box of hankies I'd just given her.

It took me a second to translate what she'd said from virus-speak to English.

"Last night? Nothing…" I replied.

"Billy nod up for doing anything?" she asked, checking I wasn't getting too friendly with him behind her sickly back.

"No – he was seeing some guys from his school," I told her. "And I phoned Chloe and the others, but no one was up for doing anything."

Sandie looked quite pleased. I think she'd have felt like she was missing out if I'd ended up spending a brilliant Saturday night out with Billy, or Chloe or Salma or any of our other friends from school. And who could blame her – I'd probably be the same if it was the other way around.

"So whad did you do?" she asked.

"I just stayed in with Dad and Tor and watched telly," I explained. "But something weird *did* happen..."

Sandie's enormous eyes seemed to light up. But maybe that was just fever.

"Whad?" she demanded through her blocked nose. "Whad happened?"

You could tell how bored she was after two days of being incarcerated at home. The remotest *hint* of something gossip-worthy had got her going.

"My dad – me and the others overheard him having this phone call. He was saying all this stuff like 'I can't wait till next time' and everything..."

"Whad – like he's been on a *date?*" she practically squealed.

Sandie loves anything remotely romantic, she really does.

"Well, me and Linn and Rowan *almost* thought he might have been out with ... with our mum."

Sandie's jaw dropped.

Like Billy, she knows the whole story to do with my mum and her disappearing trick. To everyone else at school, I just say my mum lives abroad. No one gives me a hard time about it – I guess one good thing about so many people my age coming from broken and re-modelled families means that having a mum living abroad doesn't raise anyone's eyebrows or interest too much.

"Do you really think id's your mum?" she gasped.

"Actually, no – I don't think it can be," I admitted. "It doesn't add up – she's still supposed to be out on the Cook Islands for a while. We had a letter; she *couldn't* be back..."

"Well, id's obvious, then," said Sandie, matter-of-factly.

"What is?" I frowned.

"Your dad," she continued, "is seeing someone new."

Sandie isn't what you'd normally call intuitive. When it comes to the two of us, she always shuts up and lets me do all the talking or deciding (which drives me crazy sometimes). And she was *well* off-course here; my dad seeing someone new? How ridiculous! It must be those cold germs short-circuiting her brain...

There was no *way* my dad was seeing someone new.

No *way*.

Or...

Or was there?

Chapter 5

RING, RING – WHO'S THERE?

I squinted at my plate, and tried to figure out what it was we were supposed to be eating.

It was Rowan's turn to make the Sunday tea again. How did her turn come around again so quickly? What had we done in a previous life to deserve it?

"This is—"

Dad stopped to cough.

"—lovely, Rowan. Er, what is it?"

Bless him, he always tries to pretend Rowan's efforts are edible. (I know I serve up fish fingers, spaghetti and beans with boring regularity when it's *my* turn to make meals, but at least people don't get *food* poisoning from it...)

Linn swirled her fork round in the pink sludge with a look of pure horror on her face. And she hadn't even tasted it yet.

"Is it pudding?" asked Tor.

"No," said Rowan, sitting down at her place round the kitchen table and looking slightly flustered. "Who ever heard of getting just *pudding* for tea?"

"Well, if it's not pudding, why's it pink?" Tor asked her straight out.

"It's *pink*," sighed Rowan, as if she was a world-class chef who was being questioned by a lowly punter, "because it's got *beetroot* in it."

"Beetroot's red," I pointed out.

And not unfairly, I don't think.

"I put it in the liquidizer, with natural yoghurt," Rowan explained. "To make a sauce..."

I gulped.

I had to ask the next question, if no one else would.

"To make a sauce for *what* exactly?" I asked, gingerly poking about in the lumpy pink goo with my fork.

"Roasted vegetables," she replied.

"Roasted vegetables?" said Dad, raising his eyebrows enthusiastically. "*They're* good for you!"

"And fruit," Rowan added.

"*Fruit?*" squealed Linn, spitting out her first, tentative mouthful. "What kind of *fruit*?!"

"Peaches," said Rowan defiantly. "I found a tin in the cupboard. I thought it would make it a sort of ... sweet-and-sour thing."

You know, sometimes I think Rowan stares at the fairy lights in her room too long...

Suddenly the phone shrilled out louder than

Linn's protests, and Dad went rushing out to the hall before any of us could get up off our seats to get it.

"Look – he's shut the door!" Linn hissed over the table, the terrible tea soon forgotten in the face of more secrecy on Dad's part.

"Yeah – he must be expecting this call, and doesn't want us to hear!" Rowan pointed out.

"Why not? Why doesn't he want us to hear?" Tor piped up, reminding us all that we should keep our mouths well and truly shut in his presence.

"Because it's just boring business stuff," I assured our little brother, wrinkling up my nose. "Hey – doesn't that sound like one of the cats yowling outside?"

It was smart thinking on my part – in a split-second, Tor had leapt out of his seat and tugged open the back door, heading out into the garden in search of any four-legged friend (or three-legged, in Colin's case) in need of his help.

"Listen," I whispered to my two sisters, while we had a moment to ourselves. "Sandie said something today…"

Linn rolled her eyes. At a time like this, she wasn't exactly scintillated by the notion of listening to whatever my best friend had to say – *that* was plain to see.

"What? What did Sandie say?" asked Rowan.

Bless Rowan – she's a weirdo, but at least she's a weirdo who's prepared to listen.

"Sandie said that maybe…"

I lost my nerve for a second.

"…Um, that Dad maybe has a new girlfriend," I finished off. "Maybe."

Linn and Rowan's jaws dropped till they nearly hit the hideous pink creation on their plates. But they said nothing, so they were obviously considering the idea.

"I think…"

I stared at Linn, waiting to see what she made of it all. Normally, I was quite happy for my know-all big sister to keep her opinions where the sun don't shine, but tonight, for once, I actually wanted to hear what Linn thought.

"I think," she began again, "that Sandie could be right."

Rowan looked like she might cry. She hangs out with her cool, older friends and everything, but she's all marshmallow inside, really.

"So, what do we do?" I asked Linn, hoping she had a smart answer.

"We watch and listen," said Linn, staring from me to Rowan and back again.

"Spying, you mean?" Rowan gulped.

"If that's what it takes, yes."

Linn would make a great Bond girl, she really would…

Chapter 6

I'LL TELL YOU MINE, IF YOU TELL ME YOURS

There's this kind of broad, tree-lined avenue that leads into Alexandra Palace (one of about seventy thousand ways to get into the whole park area).

It's not really open to cars, except when there's some big, fancy exhibition going on at weekends. But during the week, it's shut off as a road by these big ornate gates, with just the odd cyclist using it as a scenic short-cut, away from the traffic, or people with pooches on their way to the grassy expanses of the park.

Course, there are times of the day when the avenue – and all the old wooden benches that line it – gets busier. Like after four o'clock on week-days; that's when it becomes the unofficial snogging (and smoking) venue for loads of people from our school.

I was there this one Monday, idly wondering if the greeny-coloured, damp mould that covered the bench I was sitting on was going to stain my trousers. I was also letting my finger run along the groove of a badly carved heart, with the initials "E.K. luvs S.W." inside. I wondered if they belonged to anyone I knew. I couldn't help feeling momentarily jealous; I hate vandalism of any sort (and hacking love-hearts on park benches with a pen-knife is vandalism, I suppose) but I couldn't help wondering if there'd ever be a time when someone scratched "X.X. luvs A.L." on a lump of wood for *me*.

Though, I think I'd prefer someone more literate. Like someone who could spell "love" properly, for a start...

Now before you get the wrong idea, no, I wasn't there snogging anyone. And no, I wasn't there smoking either (please, credit me with a *brain*). I was there because the avenue is also quite a good place to hang out and gossip (usually about the people who are snogging), if you're not in the mood to hurry home.

Today, since Sandie was still lying in her snotty sickbed, I found myself sitting on a bench chatting with Kyra. Or more like *not* chatting with Kyra.

I stopped picking at the carved initials and stared at her as she checked the messages on her mobile phone. The one she was listening to seemed to be going on for ever, and whatever was being said wasn't exactly lighting up her life.

"Sorry about that," she apologized, finally clicking off her phone and slipping it back into her bag. "I was hoping for something a bit more exciting than my mum ranting on about the fifty million things I've got to pick up from the shops on the way home…"

I shrugged like I hadn't noticed how long she'd been. I wasn't really sure what to say either; the ins and outs of Kyra's relationship with her mum were still a mystery to me (all I knew was that it was bad, and that her mum had some kind of drinking problem). And since I didn't know Kyra well enough yet to go noseying into her life, I'd decided to keep stum till she told me herself. *If* she ever wanted to.

"So, I see Teresa Smith's got zero taste in men!" said Kyra, brightening up.

I looked where *she* was looking and saw Teresa Smith – only the prettiest girl in the year above us – losing her street cred with amazing speed. There, in front of anyone who cared to watch, she was holding hands and staring slushily into the eyes of some non-entity in a Muswell School for Boys uniform. It wasn't the fact that he wasn't anything special that was ruining her reputation; it was the fact that with the hand she *wasn't* holding, he was slowly and unself-consciously scratching his bum.

And not just a genteel one-finger scratch. Oh, no – this was a full-handed gouge worthy of any of the baboons down at London Zoo.

"Hope she's not going to hold *that* hand now…" I muttered to Kyra.

"It's one of those times you wish you had a video camera, isn't it?" giggled Kyra. "We could send it into that TV show; make ourselves a bit of money!"

I knew she was only joking (wasn't she?), but it didn't seem like Kyra particularly needed any extra money. Apart from living in one of the poshest turnings in Crouch End, Kyra had a few trimmings that definitely spelt "dosh", and plenty of it. Like, her phone – it wasn't any old standard mobile. It was one of those snoot, tiny ones I'd seen advertised for more money than my dad pulled in at his shop in a slow week.

Not that my dad would buy stuff like mobile phones even if he *had* the money. Technology kind of passes him by. We clubbed together and bought an answering machine for the shop one Christmas, but Dad just ended up taking it back to Argos and swapping it for a new tool box because he couldn't figure out how to work the thing. And as far as computers go, he can't get his head around websites and the Internet at all, even though Tor's tried to explain it to him loads of times.

Plenty of my friends have got their own phones and computers. It doesn't really bother me that I don't, and it doesn't bother me that the most gadgety thing in our house is a video we've had for five years (that was second-hand in the first place), mainly because I know how tough it is for Dad to keep everything together for us on his one, unspectacular wage. It doesn't bother Tor or Rowan either, but I know it *really* bothers Linn. That's why she's been frantically looking for a Saturday job – so she can start keeping herself in the style to which she'd *like* to become accustomed.

"Hey, what's up?" Kyra suddenly burst into my thoughts. "You're not drooling over Scratchy Boy, are you?"

I realized I'd had my eyes fixed a little too firmly on the bum of Teresa Smith's repulsive boyfriend for the last few seconds while I daydreamed. No wonder Kyra had got the wrong idea.

"No! No way!" I grimaced. "Disgusting geeks aren't exactly my type!"

Scruffy, I don't mind. A boy with the manners of a pig, I don't *think* so.

"So what *is* your type?" asked Kyra, narrowing her eyes at me.

We were still at that getting-to-know-you-better stage, me and Kyra. And Sandie, of course. Ever since we'd had the bust-up and make-up over the History project we'd done together, we three had all started to hang out a bit more. My other friends – Chloe, Jen, Salma and Kellie – thought me and Sandie were insane. They still reckoned that Kyra was a number-one show-off and a pain-in-the-doodah (and I understand why, since I used to see her in exactly the same way). But I'd come round to thinking that it was just a bad case of new-school nerves that made her try too hard and come over so bolshy and full-on.

"*I* don't know about what *type* of boy I go for!" I said, trying to laugh off her question.

Which was a downright lie, actually. Like most people, I can fancy all sorts of different boys for all sorts of different reasons, but I wouldn't need to do much thinking to come up with my *perfect* boy.

"Come on!" said Kyra, nudging me in the ribs with her elbow. "You tell me your type, and I'll tell you mine!"

The only person (apart from me, natch) that knew about my mega-crush on Alfie was Sandie, and I wanted it to stay that way. But what harm could this do? I could describe Alfie, without ever saying exactly who he was…

"Well," I mused, "I guess I like boys with short, messily spiky blond hair…"

"And?"

Kyra raised her eyebrows at me, egging me on.

"And light-grey eyes," I sighed. "You know – the sort that make you go a bit wobbly when you look into them, they're so spooky and pale."

"Go on!"

I didn't need much encouragement. Speaking about Alfie, even anonymously like this, was pretty much a pleasure.

"And I like guys who have great smiles. And maybe a little gold tooth somewhere at the side. That's cute. And I don't like jewellery on boys much, but you know those leather strappy bracelet things you get in Camden Market and places?"

Kyra nodded.

"Yeah, I like them," I continued, "on boys with skinny, muscular arms."

"So," said Kyra, staring at me intently now. "Who is this guy?"

"What guy?" I replied nervously. "You just told me to tell you what type I liked!"

"Come on, Ally!" she grinned. "That's not a type – that's a police photofit! You've obviously got one person in mind…"

I'm *so* transparent, I really am. I think I'm being clever and subtle and everything, but all the time I'm easier to read than a Year One ABC book.

"There's no one!" I blustered on, hoping against hope that she'd believe me. Kyra laughed out loud.

"You liar!" she giggled. "This guy sounds all right by your description, so what's the problem with him? Why can't you say who he is? What's the catch – is he only eleven or something?"

"He's four years *older* than me, actually!" I contradicted her bad-taste joke, and at the same time walked right into her trap.

"Aha! So we're getting somewhere!" shrieked Kyra, clapping her hands together as if prodding at my love life was the best game in the world. "Does he go to our school?"

"No. He goes to a sixth-form college over in Highgate…" I mumbled.

"Well? So tell!" she shrugged. "What's the point in keeping it from me?"

I couldn't think of *one* point, right at that moment, and although I thought I'd probably regret it, I ended up telling her who it was.

"His name's Alfie. He's best mates with my sister Linn," I explained, sheepishly.

"Does Linn know you fancy him?"

"God, no!" I squeaked.

The very idea made my blood run icy. Linn would *not* approve of one of her sisters fancying her best buddy – that would be far too juvenile for her. She'd never bring him around to the house ever again.

"Does he fancy you?"

"God, *no*!"

If only.

If only I could speak to him without turning into a gibbering, babbling fool, that would be a start.

"Why not? What's so weird about that?"

I was stumped. What a strange concept – Kyra honestly couldn't see why Alfie might not be interested in me. I'd spent the last few years stacking up all the reasons why someone like him could never be interested in someone like me, and now Kyra was putting a completely different spin on things.

Maybe it wasn't such a terrible idea talking to her about it after all...

"Oh – that's my phone! It could be him!"

Kyra jerked at the twittering tune jangling from her mobile, and dived into her bag to retrieve it.

I was feeling instantly deflated now that our Alfie conversation had been interrupted.

"Him who?" I asked distractedly, as I watched her practically turn her bag upside down to find her mobile.

"My new boyfriend!" Kyra grinned and whispered quickly, before she answered her phone.

Her new boyfriend?

Since when?

She hadn't even got round to telling me what *type* she went for yet, and now she had a *boyfriend*?!

Chapter 7

CUPID STRIKES AGAIN (NOWHERE NEAR ME...)

You know what was doing my head in? The fact that Kyra Davies had lived in Crouch End for about five minutes, and she'd got herself a boyfriend, just like that.

Me? I've lived here all my life, and all I've managed to chalk up is four (lousy) dates with Keith Brownlow when I was twelve and had no taste.

All the way home from the park, I couldn't help festering over how jealous I was. Not jealous of *Kyra* exactly (it wasn't like I wanted to get a voodoo doll of her and stick pins in it); just jealous of the whole idea of having a boyfriend. And that made me really mad with myself – it was so pathetic that I wanted one anyway. What was the point? My two friends who *had* had boyfriends (Salma and Jen) spent half the time they were supposed to be happily dating just moaning on about the boys, and how they never phoned when they said they would, drooled over other girls when they were out with them, and how generally useless they were. Their experience of boyfriends (as well as my *own* fleeting experience) should have put me off the whole idea.

But it didn't.

"Hello!" I shouted to no one in particular, as I barged grumpily through the front door.

I let my schoolbag drop with a clatter on to the floor and shoved my jacket on to the coat rack.

"Hello," I heard a small voice say, as I stomped past the staircase towards the kitchen, where Radio Two was blasting out some corny old song.

(Me and my sisters always retune to Radio One at breakfast, and Grandma switches it back to Radio Two when she gets in after picking up Tor from school.)

"What are you doing?" I asked, stopping to squint at my little brother.

Tor had his legs wrapped round a pole in the bannister, and was dangling backwards, his fingertips nearly touching the wooden hall floor.

"Being upside down," he stated, slightly breathlessly.

"Your face is bright red," I pointed out, turning my head around to get a better view of his beetroot-tinted features.

"Is it?" he replied, seeming quite pleased about it.

"Shout if you need a hand down," I told him, as I strolled off into the kitchen, where the smell of something good managed to lift my spirits.

Ah, the joy of Monday to Friday, when Grandma makes our tea. When everyone's guaranteed not to moan, or end up with violent indigestion.

"He's still upside down, is he?" muttered Grandma, leaning down and prodding at something in the oven.

"Yep," I said, flopping on to one of the wooden chairs around our big old table. "What's he up to?"

"They did something about bats in school today," she replied.

Well, that explained that. Tor loved animals so much that it wasn't a great surprise that he was trying to turn into one.

"What are you making, Grandma?" I asked, sniffing the air like I was one of the dogs. (Talk about *Tor* turning into an animal...)

"An aubergine and mascarpone bake."

"Huh?"

"Well, a vegetable and cheese bake, in plain English," Grandma explained, closing the oven door and straightening up. "Saw it on *Ready, Steady, Cook* the other day."

"Smells great," I nodded.

Grandma's always trying out new recipes off the

TV on us. And I'd just like to take this opportunity to personally thank all the programme controllers for putting so many cookery shows on – if it wasn't for them, our weekday teas would be a lot less interesting.

"Well, you'll just have to tell me what this one's like – I can't stay and eat with you tonight," said Grandma, peering into the small mirror beside the back door and primping up her already immaculate blondey-grey hair.

"Why – what are you doing?" I asked, while marvelling at how neat Grandma was.

Not just in the way she looked and dressed, but the way the kitchen was so spotless and ordered, even though she'd been busy throwing food together for us five seconds before. I'm the total opposite – I even manage to make a mess at breakfast. There's always sticky bits on the table where I've poured (and dribbled) orange juice, and I always have to do a toast-crumbs-in-my-hair check in the hall mirror before I leave for school.

"I'm going out..." Grandma hesitated, looking uncharacteristically flustered for a second. "I'm going on what you girls would probably call a *date*."

Well, knock me down with a vegetable and cheese bake. One minute I'm in the park with Kyra, getting told she has a boyfriend (and being deserted two seconds after she gets off the phone, 'cause she's got to meet him, and promising she'll tell me more later). Next thing I'm home, and my Grandma is telling me more or less the same thing.

"Who is he?" I demanded, feeling even more rejected and loveless now that even my sixty-year-old grandmother had pulled.

"His name's Stanley, and I met him at my friends' wedding-anniversary party a couple of weeks ago," said Grandma, matter-of-factly.

"Is he nice?" I asked, a little more warmly.

It was silly to be so grumpy with her. It wasn't her fault that *I* wasn't going out with anyone, and it wasn't as if I was going to be too jealous of her new bloke.

"Very nice. He's a retired engineer."

Yep, I definitely didn't have the hots for Stanley the retired engineer.

"So, where are you two going?" I asked, wondering if I should push it and make a joke about her being sure to get home to her flat by eleven o'clock or she'd be grounded, but Grandma looked a little too self-conscious about the whole thing to take a joke.

"Just one of the restaurants near Crouch End Broadway. I forget which one he said," muttered Grandma, wafting her hand vaguely around in the air. "Anyhow, Rowan's outside taking in the washing. Why don't you give her a hand?"

I was dismissed. Grandma had had enough of gossiping about her love life with me, that was for sure. It's funny; her and Linn are so alike. If they're done talking to you, it's like the shutters come down and that's that.

Pulling open the squeaky back door, I saw Rowan wrestling for control of a pink, flowery pair of pants with Winslet.

"Let go! Leave! I said, *leave*!" she squeaked.

But Winslet didn't *want* to leave. She'd carefully selected the pants from the mound of newly dried clothes in the laundry basket lying on the grass, and was planning on adding them to the ever-changing collection of stolen items hidden under her doggy blanket. (She may be a short, hairy, grumpy dog now, but she *has* to have been a magpie in another life – it's the only explanation.)

"Need a hand?" I asked, bending down and grabbing Winslet by the scruff of her neck.

(It's a good trick that Tor taught me: get hold of a dog or cat by the scruff and they automatically open their jaws and drop whatever's in them – toys, mice, stolen pants...)

"Thanks. Yeuchhh! *These* are going straight back in the washing machine..." said Rowan, wrinkling up her nose and holding the knickers at arm's length.

"Those are Linn's, aren't they?" I asked, peering at the floral pants.

"Oh, yeah, so they are!" said Rowan, brightening up. "Oh, well – I'm sure they'll be fine. I mean, what's a little dog saliva between friends…"

She dropped the knickers back in the pile of clean clothes and turned back to the washing line, a small, smug smile playing at her lips. Well, it's not often she manages to get one over on our bossy big sister.

"So," I began, holding out my cupped hands for Rowan to drop the pegs into. "What about Grandma having a date tonight, then?"

"Well, it's not really a big deal, is it?" Rowan shrugged. "Not compared to this stuff with Dad…"

Urgh – I'd managed to forget about that. Call me a coward (you're a coward, Ally Love), but I suddenly understood why ostriches bury their heads in the sand when trouble lurks. I'd put any thoughts about the business with Dad away in a small, dusty corner at the back of my mind, and now here was Rowan, reminding me about it all over again.

"I suppose so," I mumbled, as I half-heartedly shooed Winslet away from the laundry basket.

"Anyway, you know what Linn said about us

keeping our eyes open?" Rowan whispered, peering over my shoulder at the open back door.

"You mean, about spying on him?" I said, more frankly.

"Yeah," Rowan nodded, making the halo of tiny, metallic butterfly clips holding her dark hair off her face glint in the late-afternoon sun. "Well, I found something!"

"Like what?" I asked, bending down and grabbing Winslet by the neck.

Automatically, the thief-dog dropped one of Tor's Pokémon socks and stared ruefully up at me.

"Like, I spotted the notepad beside the phone this morning," Rowan garbled, her eyes wide and shiny with her secret. "And on it, it said 'Wednesday', with these doodles of stars all round it!"

"OK, so he must have done that when he was on the phone last night – that call where he closed the door on us…"

"Exactly!" Rowan agreed with me. "So he must be going out with *her* again on Wednesday!"

Suddenly, I realized that I didn't care about Kyra having a new boyfriend. And Grandma seeing someone was just sweet. But what I did care about very, very much was the whole idea of Dad getting romantic with someone.

Someone who *wasn't* our mum…

Chapter 8

KYRA GOES TWINKLY

"Hi, Ally," said Kyra, hurrying along the school corridor towards me. "Listen, sorry I disappeared yesterday, but I *had* to meet Ricardo."

"Ricardo? Is he Italian, then?"

I hadn't even found out his name the day before, Kyra had been so desperate to sprint off and meet Wonderboy.

"Well, his family are, way back, I suppose," Kyra shrugged, leaning up against the radiator I was parked on. "Ricardo Esposito... Sounds really nice, doesn't it?"

Kyra was looking totally twinkly-eyed. The way she'd said it I had the feeling she'd already played that game of running your name together with his. "Kyra Esposito..." nah – I wouldn't run down to the registrar's to book the wedding straight away if *I* was her.

It was the start of breaktime on Tuesday morning, and I was idly mooching around, waiting to meet up with any of my friends who happened to amble by. (Not Sandie, though – she was still at home sinking under the weight of soggy tissues and being smothered by mother love.)

"So, come on – tell me about him," I grinned. "What's he like? When did you meet him?"

I'd decided I might as well be enthusiastic about this. If I didn't have a love life of my own, I might as well get a kick out of somebody else's.

"Well—" said Kyra, her light-brown skin flushing unexpectedly.

She comes across so loud and over-confident normally that it's always a surprise when you see little chinks of shyness like that (never mind the big chunks of insecurity I know are hidden away there too).

"—I went shopping in Wood Green with my dad on Saturday, and we ended up in one of those car-phone places. Anyway, it looked like Dad was going to be in there for *ever*, so I said I'd wait for him in Burger King."

"And?"

I was intrigued. Girl Finds Love in Burger King. It didn't sound too promising...

"And Burger King was mobbed. So I spot this *really* cute lad sitting on his own at a table, and I asked if I could sit there for a while," Kyra gushed, her bushy, high ponytail bobbing as she talked. "*He* tells me he's keeping the table for his mates, but then he says of course I can sit down, if I want to!"

Amazing. If *I* saw a really cute lad sitting at an empty table, the last thing I'd do is ask to sit down. I'd never have the nerve. I'd just cower in a corner and stare longingly at him from a distance. But then maybe that's why Kyra had got herself a boyfriend and I hadn't.

"And then he asks my name, and I ask his, and we get talking... We must have been talking for about half an hour; then I look up, and see my dad coming in. So I say, 'Here's my dad – I better go', but he says, 'Quick – write down your phone number!' and shoves a serviette across the table at me. And I scribble down my number with this old eyeliner pencil I found at the bottom of my bag!"

"And he phoned you yesterday?" I asked.

"Yesterday? Huh! That was the *third* time he'd phoned me," Kyra beamed happily. "He already called on Saturday night, *and* Sunday afternoon!"

It was official: I was impressed. Compared to my one, pathetic attempt at going out with someone, this was like a Hollywood blockbuster.

"What's he like, then?" I quizzed her.

"Like I said, he's cute. He's got dark-brown hair, big brown eyes, a big cheeky smile. Looks a bit like he could be in a boy band. And he's dead chatty and funny."

So, definitely *not* like Keith Brownlow.

"When you saw him yesterday, what did you do?" I asked, raising my eyebrows at her, and getting a little cheeky myself.

"We just hung out. He jumped on a bus from his school—"

"Which school?"

Kyra frowned and glanced around like she was trying to figure out which way was north. She still hadn't been in this part of the world long enough to get the geography sorted out in her head.

"Um, can't remember the name. It's somewhere over that way, I think."

"Wood Green?" I guessed from the direction she was pointing, through a set of school walls. "I wonder which one it is…"

"Whatever," Kyra shrugged, not interested in boring details like schools. "So we just hung out for a while and talked."

"And … anything else?" I ventured.

She knew and *I* knew that we were talking snogging. It just seemed a bit tacky to come right out and say, "Did you snog, then?" even though it was the one thing I wanted to know.

"Maybe," grinned Kyra, shooting a sideways look

at me. "But anyway, best of all, we're going out properly tomorrow night!"

"Where to?"

"Skating up at Alexandra Palace."

It's good up there. Good for boy-spotting that is, not for skating. Well, very good for skating if you *can* skate – which I can't. Tor has to hold my hand and literally *drag* me round the ice whenever we go there.

"That'll be fun," I mused.

Lots of hand-holding and giggling – skating has great touchy-feely potential. Good choice, Kyra.

"But you know what's stupid?" Kyra shrugged.

"What?"

"I don't know what to wear! I mean, on Saturday, he just saw me in my old combats and a T-shirt, and yesterday I was in school uniform. Tomorrow I'd really like to look different. Y'know – really nice!"

I knew the feeling. Whenever there's a party or something, it always takes me about a week to work out what to put on. All my mates are the same, and we have this thing where we try on outfits in front of each other just to road-test them. It's a real laugh, and we always end up swapping and borrowing stuff from each other. Maybe that's what Kyra needed – a bit of the dress-rehearsal treatment...

"Well, why don't I come back to yours after school today and help you choose something?" I offered.

OK, so I had an ulterior motive: I also wanted to check out her posh house in her posh street. And maybe get a glimpse of this mother she didn't get on with.

"Uh, nah – it's OK," she said, looking suddenly ruffled. "I'll probably just shove on a jumper and my padded vest top. We're going skating, after all, so I guess it'll just have to be warm stuff…"

Did I hit a raw nerve? I wondered to myself. *Doesn't she want to have anyone back to the house?*

"Um, anyway, I better go to the loo before the bell rings," she suddenly muttered.

Ooh, it did look like she wanted to change the subject.

"OK," I shrugged. "Shall I wait for you?"

"No, it's all right," she shook her head. "You go on without me!"

I got the hint.

Just as I turned to head towards my Maths class-room, as the end-of-break bell trilled, this horrible image popped into my head: Keith Brownlow. All this love stuff had brought it back to me – i.e. our rubbish attempt at dating – when I'd done a really good job of forgetting it for a long, long time.

You see, it started in that way that it often does in real life, and never, *ever* in movies. Keith Brownlow was this kind of cute-looking boy in a crowd of lads in the year above me. Then one day, out of the blue, one of his mates comes over and says, "My mate Keith fancies you. Do you want to go out with him?"

Now, I did a stupid thing: I was *so* flattered that someone cute-looking (and in the year above!) was interested in little old me, that I persuaded myself in two seconds flat that I was madly in love with him.

And so me and Keith Brownlow went out four times (twice, we just hung around the park; once, we went to Pizza Hut; and once, I watched him play football and hung out with him afterwards).

And it was all a horrible disaster. Partly, it was my fault, because I was spending all my time trying to persuade myself that I fancied him, when I didn't really. The rest was his fault – I mean, he may have looked cute, but he hardly ever *talked*. Every time I saw him, I ended up babbling like crazy, and all he'd do was grunt in reply. And I should never have let him kiss me. To be honest, I didn't even know he was going to *do* it. One minute he was hovering outside my gate, slugging on his Coke, after walking me home (in silence) from the football match. Next thing I know, he's lunged at me, suctioned his lips on to mine, and done that unforgettable burp, right in my mouth. Talk about a memorable first kiss.

I think he knew he'd blown it then. I scurried inside the house after he walked me home and hoped against hope that he'd never phone me or come near me again, and luckily he didn't. We'd both done this thing ever since, where we never looked at each other at school. Maybe it was juvenile, but it was a lot easier to pretend we'd never met than to remind ourselves what a huge, embarrassing mistake it was.

I shook the memory out of my head and tried to concentrate on where I was going. Right now, there were about a million people coming down the stairs that I was trying to go up, to get to my Maths class.

"Don't push!" I yelled, as this surge of Year Seven boys came towards me.

But of *course* they took no notice of me, and of *course* they kept on pushing. Next thing, I'm on the floor, with everything in my bag spilt everywhere.

I was just thanking my lucky stars that I'd decided to wear trousers and not a skirt that day (landing on your bum in full view of loads of people is bad enough – having your skirt over your head at the same time would be just *shameful*), when something made me look up.

Stepping over my scattered books right at this second was the one, the only, Keith Brownlow. He was doing our trick, I noticed, as I scrambled, red-faced, to my feet. He was staring down at the tiled floor and pretending he couldn't see me.

Phew.

And then I spotted what he was actually staring at.

The little blue box I kept in my bag had burst open, and my tampons were fanning out across the shiny red floor tiles...

Nice one, Ally! I told myself, wondering if I should just ram my empty bag over my head and make like an ostrich.

Chapter 9

SPEAKING IN DISGUISE

I was sitting at one end of the sofa, with my school books spread all around me, when Linn came bustling into the living room.

(Grandma had left ten minutes before, which is why I had my homework with me in the living room instead of upstairs at my desk. She's got this pet theory that you can't study properly in the same room as a TV; and to be honest, she's right. Instead of doing anything remotely swotty, I was gazing blankly at some holiday programme, while simultaneously reliving my humiliation in front of Keith Brownlow the previous day and stroking Colin the cat, who was gently snoring on top of my opened textbook.)

"I just saw Dad come out of the bathroom..." Linn hissed, scooting over and shifting some of my books so she could sit down.

At Linn's pronouncement, Rowan roused herself from flicking through her magazine. And Tor stopped playing his game of Spin the Bottle on the floor (which consisted of him hugging Rolf or Winslet, depending on where the empty plastic Coke bottle ended up pointing).

"...and he's done his hair all fancy!"

It was Wednesday night – the night we girls were primed to watch out for signs of Dad going out again. And you didn't get much more of a sign than Dad doing his hair.

"He's greased it back?" I asked, feeling my heart rate pick up.

For a long, long time we'd only ever seen it as short-ish, curly-ish and style-free. But years ago – and we had the photographic evidence in the albums in cupboard – he always wore it smoothed back, all slick and shiny like the teddy boys did in the fifties. That's what had first made our mum and dad fancy each other; they were both really into fashion – only fashion that was several *decades* out of date. Dad had this kind of rockabilly style, with his greased hair and checked shirts, worn with turned-up jeans and Doc Marten boots. Mum's style was straight out of the seventies, with her long wavy hair, velvet jackets and hippie dresses. They must have made a weird couple. But cool too, I think.

So Dad's retro hairdo *had* to mean something. He'd done it like that the previous week when he'd disappeared off for the pint or two with his "plumber mate" – but strangely enough, he hadn't said anything about going out tonight. Only the scribble on the phone pad had given that away.

"He's coming down the stairs!" whispered Rowan, hearing the thudding of footsteps a microsecond before the rest of us.

We must have looked like dress-shop dummies when Dad came into the room. Rowan, Tor, Linn and I were silently and stiffly glued to the TV, as if the story about scenic coach-trips for the over-sixties was just about the most fascinating thing we'd ever seen.

"Um, listen, I forgot to say..." said Dad, hovering in the doorway, awkwardly. "I'm just going out for a couple of hours. Just ... popping out for a pint."

"With the plumber?" I asked, hoping I looked innocent.

"Um ... yes, with the plumber. Jake, yeah..."

He didn't sound too convincing. And he didn't *look* too convincing either. He was wearing his best white shirt, and both it and his jeans were ironed, if I wasn't very much mistaken. What bloke would iron jeans (that were never normally anywhere within an eight-kilometre radius of an iron), just to go to the pub with a mate?

"Sorry, guys," he apologized. "I should have checked with you first. None of you are going out are you? Is someone OK to look after Tor?"

"Of course!"

"Yes!"

"Sure!"

The colliding voices of his three daughters must have caught Dad by surprise. I don't think he'd ever heard us sound so definite when it came to babysitting duties.

"Well, all right. Thanks, you lot," he said sheepishly, as he disappeared into the hall. "I won't be late!"

Linn darted over to the window as soon as we heard the front door shut.

"OK, he's gone," she said, ventriloquist-style through clenched teeth, as she smiled and waved Dad off.

She spun round, ready to talk over events with us, when something made her stop.

"What's happening?" asked Tor, narrowing his eyes at all three of us.

Tor – we'd forgotten about him in all the intrigue. He'd silently listened to us gossiping about the business of Dad's hair, and he'd played along with keeping quiet and watching the telly when Dad had walked in the room. But really, he hadn't a clue what we were all up to – and we wanted it to stay that way. After all, the night before, he got kind of worked up when Dad and us had been joking around about Grandma's hot date (we knew he was worked up because he didn't make his food into any shapes before he ate it, like he normally does). We finally got it out of him that he was scared Grandma wouldn't love him as much if she had a boyfriend. And if he was scared of *that*, then we sure didn't want him freaking out about Dad seeing someone else…

"We're just taking the mickey out of Dad, that's all," I tried to reassure him. "Just 'cause he's putting all that slimy gel in his hair!"

"It's wax, actually," he corrected me, earnestly.

You've got to watch it with kids sometimes; they're smarter than you think.

"Hey, do you suppose I should run after Dad?" asked Linn, trying to sound normal but staring meaningfully at me and Rowan. "You know – to check he's got his *keys*?"

It suddenly clicked – we were about to have a conversation in code. Me and my sisters sometimes do this when we want to keep stuff well over Tor's head. (And Grandma's, now and again. There *are* times when you don't want your gran to know *everything* that you're up to.) According to the code so far, Linn was letting me and Rowan know that she planned to follow Dad and see where he was going … and who he was *really* meeting.

I glanced over at Rowan to make sure she'd sussed the code thing – sometimes she's too busy being an airhead to notice what's going on. But Rowan shot me a quick look back and I knew we were all on the same wavelength.

"That's a good idea!" I nodded at my eldest sister. "We might be in bed by the time Dad comes back, so he'll need his keys to get in!"

(Translation: "Go for it, Linn!")

"But he *took* his keys!" Tor piped up, before Linn could head for the door.

"Er, no he didn't!" said Rowan.

"He *did*! He was jingling them in his hand!"

Never underestimate the observational skills of a seven year old.

"Was he?" I smiled at Tor, "Well, that was clever of you to notice."

Annoying, more like.

Me, Rowan and Linn were silent for a second, stumped, now that our first attempts at proper spying had been stalled.

"Oh, I think I'll go to the shop!" Rowan burst out, scrambling out of the armchair. "I really fancy … some … Wine Gums!"

(Translation: "Now that Linn's plan is down the dumper, I've tried to come up with an alternative excuse to get out of the house and follow Dad.")

"*Grrandma* says Wine Gums stick in your teeth and rot them," Tor squinted at Rowan dubiously.

"Well … maybe I just fancy having rotten teeth, OK?" Rowan shrugged, searching the floor for her shoes.

(Translation: "Leave me alone, Tor – I know it's lame but it was the first stupid thing that came into my head!")

"You'd better hurry, Ro – the shop might close!" said Linn sternly.

(Translation: "Hurry up if you're going, or you'll never catch up with Dad!")

"But the shop stays open past my bedtime!" Tor chipped in.

I gritted my teeth together and knew my sisters would be doing the same. It was like living with a junior member of MI6.

"I think the shop is closing early tonight. I'm sure I saw a sign in the window saying that…" I tried to pacify him.

(Translation: "Tor, we love you but shut up and let us lie to you!")

"I can't find my other shoe!" whined Rowan,

knowing that time was ticking away. "Winslet – have you taken it?"

(Translation: "I'll never catch up with Dad at this rate, because that stupid dog's hidden my shoe under a bed somewhere!")

"Ro, listen: forget the Wine Gums," Linn sighed, shoving her hands on her hips. "You can get them another day."

(Translation: "Give up. Dad'll be *well* gone. We'll try another time when Inspector Tor isn't listening in.")

Tor glanced around and seemed to notice that all of us were deflated for some reason or other, and he didn't like it.

Since I was the only one still sitting, he fixed on me.

"Winslet would like a cuddle," said Tor, struggling to pick up and carry the reluctant, hairy sausage of a dog over to the sofa, and scrambling up next to me with her.

(Translation: "Tor would like a cuddle.")

And who was I to refuse those big brown eyes. (Tor's, I mean, not Winslet's...)

Chapter 10

LOVE AND CHIPS

I know I moan about Linn, but she was really cool when Billy phoned and begged me to come out and see a movie with him before his brain exploded with boredom.

OK, so it was obvious that it didn't need all of us to stay home and look after Tor while Dad was out with ... well, *whoever*, but in the circumstances, I felt like I should be there, showing solidarity with my sisters.

But as soon as I came back in the living room and said how I'd told Billy I couldn't come out, she'd told me not to be so silly and to get back on the phone and tell him I'd meet him up at Muswell Hill Odeon in half an hour.

And so here I was, sitting in the darkness next to Billy, nudging him to pass me the giant bucket of popcorn he was hogging.

The only problem was, the new sci-fi movie we were meant to be seeing (Billy's choice) was sold out. So we'd been forced to give up until another day, or opt for this romantic comedy thing that was starting around the same time. And since neither of us was in the mood to go home (me, because I'd just worry about what my dad was up to; Billy because, well, he was plain *bored*) we stuck it out.

"Ally, how come that girl keeps on crying?" Billy whispered loudly, pointing up at the screen as I wrestled the bucket of popcorn from his other hand.

"Because she loves that blond guy," I whispered back, "but she thinks she doesn't stand a chance with him."

Boys aren't too sharp at picking up emotional stuff, are they?

"Oh, OK…" Billy nodded, but sounded unconvinced. "But how come the bloke with the blond hair keeps being horrible to her?"

"Because he loves *her*, but he's trying to hide it."

Even in the semi-dark, I could see Billy frowning. This film wasn't doing much for his understanding of the intricate ways of romance. And who could blame him for struggling with it? After all, the two characters we were watching would spend an hour and a half going through a whole pile of complicated misunderstandings, but just before the credits rolled – shazam! – they'd come to their senses, realize how in love they were and live happily ever after. And surprise, surprise, life's not like that. (If it was, after all these years of fumbling, blushing conversations and awkward silences, me and Alfie would be well on our way to announcing our engagement or something by now.)

"I don't get it – who's this other guy *here*?" asked Billy, forgetting to whisper now, which must have been just fantastic for the people sitting around us.

"He's her boss. He's in love with her too."

While I was trying to explain the film's ludicrous romantic entanglements to Billy, for a fleeting second, I thought not of Dad and his mystery date, but of the other hot date that was going on – Kyra and Ricardo, slip-sliding their way around Ally Pally ice rink.

I immediately shoved the thought to the back of my mind. The best *I* could do with my Wednesday night was explain storylines to my dense mate. And speaking of that, it suddenly struck me that I'd just learnt an important life lesson, which is: only attempt to watch romantic movies with a) girl mates, or b) boyfriends. Girl mates are always up for a good chick flick, and boyfriends will at least *pretend* to like them, for the sake of their girl-friends. But romantic movies and single boys don't mix – it brings out the worst, most cynical streak in them.

Basically, watching a romantic film with a boy who *isn't* your boyfriend is just *asking* for trouble.

"*Burrrrrrrrrrrrrrrrrrrp!* Oooh, sorry!" sniggered Billy.

As the tutting started behind us, I slunk so low I practically slipped off my seat...

OK, another life lesson is *not* to tell Billy anything vaguely important and expect a useful answer.

"But you don't know for *definite*!" said Billy, through a mouthful of tomato-sauce- and (blee!) mayonnaise-drenched chips.

We were strolling along Muswell Hill Broadway, heading towards my bus stop. I had been a bit dubious about telling Billy what was going on with Dad, but for some strange reason (I think the film was so bad in the end that it turned my brain to mush) I told him everything that was rattling around in my muddled head.

The reason that I *hadn't* planned on telling him was the fact that he's not too brilliant with "sensitive" stuff. (Put it this way: he isn't Sandie, who's so sensitive that she can cry at *car ads* on the telly, if they're slushy enough.) Here's an example: there was this one time, years ago, when I got a bit upset at how long Mum had been gone, and all Billy did was go very quiet, then tell me I could borrow his Gameboy for an unlimited period if I wanted. I mean, OK, so it was really sweet, bless him, but a girl buddy would give you a hug, wouldn't they?

(Actually ... you know something? There I am moaning on, but I've suddenly just remembered that I was quite chuffed at the time. I'd never had a go at a Gameboy before and within one minute of playing on it, I'd got totally addicted and managed to forget about Mum for a bit. Maybe Billy isn't so useless after all. And maybe I'm just a bit of an ungrateful moo...)

But anyway, as we queued at the fish and chip shop opposite the Odeon, common sense was telling me that I should stick to talking about how much he'd hated the movie (loads); how much his school was bugging him (loads); if he still had a crush on the eighteen-year-old girl who'd moved in next door to him (most definitely); the usual stuff. But instead, I blurted. Well, Billy and I have known each other since we were little kids, so it's hard *not* to tell him what's going on. Even if he generally doesn't have anything remotely helpful to say about it.

"What do you mean, I 'don't know for definite'?" I asked, wondering how he had room in his skinny body for the mound of chips he was stuffing his face with. He'd already hoovered up *triple* his fair share of popcorn in the cinema.

"Well, you don't know for *certain* that your dad is out on a date with a woman," Billy shrugged.

"What are you saying – that he's out on a date with a *man*?"

I know I was deliberately misunderstanding him, but I was a bit irked at Billy's unwillingness just to go with what I was telling him.

"No! I don't mean that. It's just that I think maybe you've got it wrong!"

"Look, Billy," I said, regretting that I'd ever opened my mouth, "I think I know my own father pretty well, and I know when something weird is going on!"

"Yeah, but I still think you're overreacting!" he mumbled, as he rammed more chips in his mouth. "I mean, my mum and dad go out all the time, and *I* don't know what they're up to. They're just out – like tonight – *doing* stuff."

"Billy – you can't compare me and my dad to you and your parents!"

"Why not?" he blinked at me, looking slightly hurt.

I couldn't feel sorry for him, though. Not while he had this disgusting dribble of tomato sauce oozing down his chin.

"It's totally different!" I tried to explain. "Dad is really close to all of us – we all know what's going on in our family!"

Well, that wasn't quite true. None of us knew what Dad was up to this particular evening; *that* was the problem.

"So, what are you saying – that I'm not close to my mum and dad?" asked Billy, coming to a halt beside my bus stop.

"Well, you're not, are you?"

It wasn't like Billy and his folks didn't get on – it was just that they all drifted about in their biggish house, all doing their own thing. Whenever I went round there, Billy's mum was always popping out to her coffee mornings and the garden centre and her evening classes. And his dad was always the same – saying a cheery hello to me and then burying his head in the paper for the rest of the time.

"We *are* close!" Billy protested.

"Billy – you don't even know what your dad does for a *living*!"

"I – I do! He works for … an insurance company!"

"Doing *what* exactly, Billy?" I tested him, my hands on my hips.

Boys are rubbish at knowing important details. They really are.

"Uh..."

Billy was saved by the fact that my bus drew up just then, opening its doors with a swish of hydraulics.

"See you up the park on Sunday, if I don't talk to you before!" he yelled, as the doors swooshed closed behind me.

I felt a bit mean going on like that at Billy, and tried to make it up by hurtling up to the top deck and waving at him like mad before the bus whizzed round the roundabout and dipped down the steep hill towards Crouch End.

As Billy waved his greasy fingers back at me, the bus driver did the usual kamikaze trick of hurtling down the forty-five-degree incline at an alarming rate, hurtling me bum-first down on to the seat. Normally, I hate this part of the journey (I tend to play out a whole morbid scenario in my mind: the screech of brakes, the bus tilting over, the local-paper headline, "Bus Careers Out Of Control On Perilous Hill – All Passengers Horribly Squashed"), but tonight I quite enjoyed the sensation. With the top of the bus to myself and the carpet of lights of London spread out down below, it was kind of like being on a Disneyland ride.

I was almost disappointed when the bus finally squealed to a halt by the junction at the bottom of the hill. But just as I stuck my feet up on the back of the seat in front and relaxed, something caught my eye.

The couple huddling in the bus shelter on the other side of the road were doing some seriously steamy snogging. It was better than anything in the film I'd just watched, that was for sure. I squinted for a better look; the way they were going, it was like a cross between mouth-to-mouth resuscitation and a WWF wrestling competition.

It was at that second that a passing car illuminated the couple in the glare of its headlights. Although I couldn't see her face, I recognized the girl's high, bushy ponytail instantly.

Oh. My. God. What was Kyra Davies *like*?!

Chapter 11

DAD SLIPS UP

"He's whistling!" whispered Rowan, as if Dad whistling first thing in the morning was the wildest thing to happen in our house all year.

Rowan was attacking some bread on the worktop, waving the long breadknife at me ominously as she made her point.

"So?" I whispered back, as I grabbed myself a glass out of the cupboard.

Speaking of wild things, Rowan's hair would've scored a definite nine out of ten on any wild scale this morning. She had it done up in two short plaits (nothing wrong with that), but the bottom of her plaits were tied with whole streamers of different coloured ribbons that trailed down over her white school shirt. If she stood still for too long, she was in danger of having small kids use her as a maypole.

"*So*, if he's whistling like that, maybe it means he's happy. You know, maybe he had a good time last night!"

I heard what Rowan was saying, but I glanced

over my shoulder to check that Tor hadn't. Luckily, we had the radio up loud and Tor was pretty much absorbed in carving his toast into something specific.

"Ro, whistling doesn't mean anything. We need more to go on than that..."

Rowan looked a little huffy with me. She grabbed the mound of bread she'd just cut (all squint), turned and plonked it down on the table.

"Hi, guys!" Dad's voice suddenly boomed above the radio.

"Hi, Dad!" said Rowan, Tor and I, simultaneously.

"Ah," exclaimed Dad, settling into his usual chair at the table, and rubbing his stomach. "Pass me some of that bread, Ally Pally – I'm starving!"

At that point, Linn breezed into the kitchen, looking as immaculate and ironed as she always does.

By contrast, an uncomfortable damp sensation made me look down at the cuff of my own white school shirt, which was currently soaking up a pool of orange juice right by my plate. I yanked my arm up and sucked at the cloth, and wished – for a split-second – that I was just slightly *less* of a clumsy geek and slightly *more* like Linn. (And you don't hear me say that too often...)

"What's this about being starving?" smiled Linn, bending over to peck a kiss on Dad's forehead before she sat down. "What have you been up to that's made you so hungry, Dad? Bit of a night last night, was it?"

Good one, Linn! I thought proudly, as my big sister launched today's offensive before she'd even had any cornflakes.

"No, no," Dad shook his head, concentrating intently on buttering his wonky slice of bread. "Quiet night, really. Few drinks, and a bit of chat. That's all."

"What pub did you go to, Dad?" asked Rowan, getting in on the act.

"Um, it was just that one off the Broadway," he muttered, vaguely.

I watched Rowan open her mouth and then close it again. She was obviously just about to question him about which of the many pubs off the Broadway that he meant exactly, when she realized she might incriminate herself. (I guessed Rowan didn't *really* want Dad knowing what me and Linn already knew – that she'd been in most of those pubs at one time or another, thanks to hanging out with her two best mates, who were both eighteen.)

My turn.

"So how's Jake?" I asked, studying Dad to see if he'd give himself away.

"Jake?"

A hint of a puzzled frown crossed Dad's face.

Aha! Got him... I thought, desperate to glance over at my sisters and check that they'd spotted that too.

"Oh, Jake! Yes, fine," Dad attempted a recovery. "Yes, Jake's ... OK."

Yeah, *right*. And just how long have you had this imaginary friend, Mr Love?

"And what did you two talk about, then?" I continued, practically giddy now that I was sure we'd caught Dad out in his lie.

"Um, just ... sport. That kind of thing," he said casually.

To add weight to his casual act, Dad picked up the marmalade jar and pretended to be fascinated by the wording on the label. Who was he kidding? And what was with the "sport" conversation? Dad watched cycling stuff like the Tour de France on telly, but beyond that he knew as much about sport as he did about the nutritional value of marmalade.

"Don't we have any *normal* stuff?" Tor suddenly interrupted, while trying to ram a piece of bread that lurched from being ten centimetres thick at one side to a sliver at the other into the toaster.

"Sliced? No we've run out. We've only got that," said Rowan slightly tersely, feeling her culinary skills were being criticized once again, even if it was only bread in question.

"But I can't finish what I'm making with this!" Tor whined, flopping the bread in the air.

"What *are* you making, Tor?" I asked, squinting at the carved piece of toast already on his plate.

Tor trotted back to his place at the table and put the toast up to his face.

"Cool!" mumbled Rowan, nodding at the sight of the Chris Evans style (toast) specs our brother was balancing on the bridge of his nose.

"I needed more toast for the arms!" Tor explained, looking at us all through the holes he'd so expertly cut out, while pointing at the space between his home-made glasses and his ears.

The technical specifications of his work of art were certainly making our normally monosyllabic little brother very chatty this morning. I was just about to quiz him on how he'd planned to *fix* the arms to the rest of the edible specs when a screech from Dad's chair alerted me to the fact that he was on the move.

"Where are you going?" asked Linn, seeing our prey slip away.

"Um, I just remembered there's an early delivery

due at the shop this morning," said Dad, heading out of the kitchen armed with his bread and marmalade. "Better get round there now..."

"Damn!" muttered Linn, under her breath.

"I *heard* that..." muttered Tor, disapprovingly.

So, we got nothing out of Dad. But luckily, *someone* was willing to talk – and tell all. Even if it was on a totally different subject.

"...and then he was skating *straight* towards me, and I was screaming and everything, but he *deliberately* crashes straight into me, grabbing me and cuddling me." Kyra giggled at the memory. "And we were laughing like mad, and then he says, 'I'm freezing – do you fancy warming me up?' And *I* said, 'Sure – you want me to buy you a coffee from the machine?' Geddit?"

I got it. So much for Kyra giving a cool back-hander to his saucy line; it sure looked like they were doing a good job of warming each other up when *I* saw them the night before – and that was what I was *really* interested in hearing about. I still hadn't quite got over the shock of seeing Kyra and Ricardo re-enacting a scene out of some steamy movie, specially since the setting was a bus shelter on the W7 bus route.

To be honest, I wasn't exactly blown away by

the sound of Ricardo's unsubtle charms, but I was having quite a good time listening to Kyra's tales, or at least as much as she could squeeze into the short journey along the corridor between English and Maths classes.

"And he definitely wants to see me again!" gushed Kyra, her upturned nose crinkling as she grinned, so that her sprinkling of freckles disappeared. "He's asked me to go to his mate's party in Muswell Hill with him on Saturday!"

"Yeah?" I said dolefully, a sinking feeling suddenly washing over me, so that I totally forgot to tease her about the bus-stop snog-fest.

"What's wrong?" asked Kyra, scanning my face.

"Nah, it's nothing," I tried to laugh, thankful that the door of the Maths class was looming up and I'd be spared any further explanation of my Party Complex.

So I didn't want to tell Kyra about it there and then ('cause I didn't want to sound like the pathetic, sorry-for-myself geek I know I can be), but basically, *this* is my Party Complex: hearing about a party that you *know* you're going to get an invite to is exciting. Hearing about a party that you're *not* going to get an invite to is just sheer torture.

I mean, parties can be rubbish, can't they? But

there's always that potential; the potential to have a brilliant laugh with your mates, to meet new people, to meet new boys... (Uh-oh, I'm off on the boy thing again.)

But that's the problem with hearing about parties and knowing you're not invited – all that potential is going on and you're stuck at home playing Junior Scrabble with your little brother while your kleptomaniac dog keeps running off with random vowels.

OK, I'm speaking about myself here, but you get my drift.

"Anyway, I'll keep you posted!" Kyra grinned at me conspiratorially, before she darted off to her own class.

"Yeah, keep me posted on what fantastic things are happening next in your charmed life, Kyra," I mumbled grumpily.

Chapter 12

STUNNED? ONLY A *HUGE* BIT...

"Yeeeeooooowww!"

Grandma, who was busy pulverizing some potatoes into submission with a masher, shot me this look that said, "I told you so!"

And she was right. When you've got an old coffee jar (painted bright blue with paper stars stuck on it – one of Rowan's early artistic efforts) that's stuffed with kitchen utensils, it's really dumb to try to turn the fishcakes you're frying just with your fingers.

I was just about to run my stinging hand under the cold-water tap, when I heard the phone ring in the hall.

"I'll get it!" I yelled, hurrying through to grab the receiver.

I presumed it would be Sandie; she was going to phone me back once she'd had a think about what video I should bring round with me on Saturday night. I'd called her as soon as I'd got in from school to see how she was getting on with her pet virus. Her horrible cold had turned into some even more horrible gastric thing, and she'd been confined to her little pink bedroom for the entire week by both her doctor and her mother. She was now going completely round the bend after days' and days' worth of mollycoddling (her mother was asking for regular updates on the state of her "bowel movements" for goodness' sake), and was desperate for me to come and inject some normality in to her life. ("Do you want me to bring anything?" I'd asked her. "Just a video. Oh, and maybe you could get me something from the hardware shop too." "What?" I asked, wondering if the virus had affected her brain. "One of those big industrial padlocks," she sighed. "So I can lock my stupid mother out of my room...")

"Hello?" I said down the phone, suddenly aware that I could smell something fishy at close quarters...

"Can I speak to Ally, please?" said a voice that wasn't Sandie's, but that *was* vaguely familiar.

"Yeah, it's me," I replied, sniffing at the hand that was holding the phone and sussing out that it was the one I'd been flipping the fishcakes with. Poo.

I cradled the receiver awkwardly, between my head and neck, and – using my non-burnt, non-smelly hand – lifted a corner of my shirt and wiped away the grease from the plastic handle.

"Oh, hi! I thought it was maybe one of your sisters," I heard the girl's voice say, as I transferred the phone to my other ear with my clean hand.

"Kyra?" I said, clicking who it was.

"Yeah, it's me! What are you up to?"

"Not much…" I shrugged, holding my greasy, fishy-fingered hand well away from me.

What could I tell her? That after I heard that she was going to a party on Saturday night with her new boyfriend, I spent the whole of Maths feeling particularly hacked off? And then I'd walked home from school (feeling particularly hacked off); tried to do my homework but couldn't concentrate (because I was too hacked off); phoned Sandie on her sickbed to see if I could come round and see her on Saturday night (so I wouldn't be the only one hacked off at not going to a party); and finally that I'd nearly deep-fried my hand because I was too hacked off to pay attention when my grandmother told me to use a spatula instead of risking third-degree burns?

"Hey, listen, Ally," said Kyra. "I've got a bit of a proposition for you…"

I was intrigued…

"Like what?"

"Do you remember what I told you at school

today? About Ricardo's mate having a party on Saturday?"

Did I remember? The fact was only *seared* into my brain…

"Yes, the party. I remember something about that…" I mumbled, trying to sound like I couldn't care less.

"Well, do you fancy coming?"

A wave of happiness steamrollered over me. I wanted to scream "YES, PLEASE!!", but I decided very quickly that that would not rate too highly on a cool scale.

"Uh, yes – sure, I'd like to come!" I squeaked, instead.

(While a small voice in my head was also shouting, "And what about Sandie?" and I was doing a wonderful job of ignoring it…)

"Great!" said Kyra. "Only there *is* a catch…"

Isn't there always?

"What is it?" I frowned, becoming aware of a rasping sensation on my fingers.

I glanced up and saw Colin the cat, perched on a stair at shoulder-level to me, stretching his neck through the bannisters and enthusiastically licking my fishcake-scented fingers.

"It's like this," Kyra began. "I was just talking to Ricardo on the phone, and he was saying that he wants to bring this mate of his along to the party too, so I said, 'Well, can I bring *my* mate as well?' "

Me. *I* was her mate. And if I wasn't very much mistaken, I was just about to have my very first blind date.

"—and Ricardo says, 'Hey, it'll be like *Blind Date*!' "

Kyra didn't look much like Cilla Black, but I can't say I cared. And I know blind dates can sometimes be a disaster, but on the boy front, it was the best offer I'd had all year. And in a week where I'd not only made a fool of myself in front of Alfie, but also in front of the only boy I'd ever been out with too, I kind of thought I deserved a change of luck.

"No problem. It could be a laugh," I giggled, trying to keep the wobble of hysteria in my voice under control.

Wait till I tell Chloe and the others at school tomorrow! I thought frantically. *Wait till I tell Sandie! Er, on second thoughts...*

I was debating whether to phone Billy and boast about it, or leave it till I saw him on Sunday to blurt my news out, when Kyra wrapped up the call pretty suddenly.

"Oh, gawd ... my mum's just come in. I've got to go. Speak to you at school tomorrow!"

And with a clatter from her end she was gone.

Slowly, I put the receiver down and walked back into the kitchen in a daze, only narrowly avoiding falling over Colin, who was weaving (make that *hopping*) his way around my legs, in the vain hope that I was carrying any spare fish in one of my pockets.

"All right, Ally?" asked Grandma, giving me one of her X-ray looks.

She must have thought I was ill, the way I was wandering about like a zombie. Probably thought I'd contracted Sandie's Horrible Thing.

"Grandma – I've got a date on Saturday!" I blurted out.

"Have you, dear? Well that makes two of us!" she smiled brightly, clattering plates on the table.

"Stanley again?" I asked, remembering her dinner date earlier in the week.

"Of course it's Stanley. What do you think I am, some wanton woman going out with two men in the same week?" she said, brusquely. "And who are you going out with?"

I didn't take offence at the brusque business – it's just the way Grandma talks. Mum isn't like that, though; she's more ditzy, like Rowan (well, from what I remember). It's funny how it kind of skipped a generation, with Linn ending up like a mini-clone of Grandma.

"That's the thing," I said, responding to Grandma's question. "I don't know his name. Well, not yet."

"Blind date, is it?" Grandma frowned. "You're not meeting him on your own, are you?"

"No, I'm going out in a foursome with my friend Kyra. This lad's a mate of her boyfriend's."

I felt myself blushing as I explained it to her. I was probably going to spend the next two days blushing about it. I'd be luminous *red* by the time I finally got introduced to this boy. He'd probably think I had some strange tropical disease and insist on a note from my doctor before he'd go anywhere near me.

"Hello, girls! What are you two gossiping about?" said Dad, coming into the kitchen and scooping Colin up into his arms and away from my legs.

"Nothing much," shrugged Grandma.

She's great that way. She knows when there's things that we might not want to tell Dad about. I mean, I *would* tell Dad before I went out on Saturday, but only once I'd stopped being a gibbering, girlie wreck about it.

"Well, it didn't sound like that to me!" Dad

grinned, standing in the middle of the kitchen in his bare feet, oldest faded jeans, scruffiest black T-shirt and with the purriest cat in his arms.

And with his hair normal and curling, he didn't look anything like he had done the night before, when he'd seemed so smartened up (for *him*, I mean; my dad's not exactly the kind of guy you'd ever see in a suit...).

"Just girls' talk, Martin," said my Grandma, in that tone of hers that means "that's it – you're not getting any more explanation than that!".

"Oh, that's right!" he teased us. "Just you two keep your little secrets from me!"

"Ah, now, speaking of keeping things from you – I nearly forgot," said Grandma, glancing up at him from fixing the table. "Someone rang earlier, when you and Tor were out feeding the rabbits in the garden. I was going to come and get you, but she told me not to bother."

She?

At the mention of that one word – that one *pronoun*, if we're going to get pernickety – I came out of my date-induced walking coma.

"Er, who – who was that, then?" asked Dad, looking suspiciously sheepish.

"Sorry, can't remember her name. I should have written it down," said Grandma, clattering the forks and knives into place. "All I remember is the message."

"And that was…?" asked Dad, his voice sounding ever so slightly strangled.

"If you're still up for Sunday, then give her a call. Does that make sense?"

Grandma looked up at Dad with her steely grey eyes.

"Uh … yep. Yes – that makes sense. Oooh, smells like tea's nearly ready. I better give everyone a shout!"

Dad – and Colin – were out of the kitchen door at the speed of light.

I looked at Grandma.

She looked back at me.

I saw her fractionally raise one eyebrow and, in that unspoken second, *I* knew that *she* knew that *I* knew that *she* knew *something* was going on.

If you see what I mean…

Chapter (13)

SMALL, BUT SMART

We were just heading out of the doorway of the pet shop when Tor tugged at my sleeve.

"The parrot!" he whispered to me, his eyes wide and earnest.

I glanced back at the shop's resident grey parrot, whose cage stood above the cash desk.

"What *about* the parrot?" I asked, ducking to one side to let another customer in.

"He said my name!" gasped Tor.

Tor does this thing, where – after we've chosen what we need to keep our menagerie going – *I* do the dull stuff like queuing up to pay, while *he* talks Tor-talk to the mice and hamsters in their cages. He also tries to bond with the resident parrot by giving it long, meaningful stares.

I thought about it for a second as I hustled Tor out of everyone's way and pointed him in the general direction of the café a couple of doors along. Call me cynical, but to me, the sound the bird made was your basic "squawwwk!" type parrot noise. But I guess it *could* sound a bit like "Torrrrr!".

If you stuck your fingers in your ears and hummed a bit, that is.

Still, who was I to burst Tor's bubble?

"Wow! He said your name? That's cool!" I nodded down at Tor, putting my hand firmly on his back and steering him into Shufda's.

As we waited for our two hot chocolates – a regular treat after our Saturday-morning pet-shop expedition – Tor took out the new goldfish scoop-net we'd just bought from the plastic bag and proceeded to capture the salt cellar with it.

"Watch you don't knock it over, Tor," I whispered.

Tor's a good kid – you can take him most places and never be embarrassed by him, unlike a lot of other children. Even when he was really little he was kind of laid-back. Other two year olds would be having screaming hissy fits on the bus because they weren't being allowed to eat the bus ticket or something, and Tor would just stare at them with his big, brown eyes, like he was trying to figure out what their problem was.

"I'm being careful!" he assured me, as the waiter came over with two steaming mugs.

"OK. So how've things been at school this week?

Are you friends with Freddie again?"

I liked these chats we had on our own. I mean, I always did most of the chatting (no surprise), but it was still pretty nice, just the two of us.

"Uh-huh," nodded Tor, licking chocolatey froth off his spoon.

"What was it you two were fighting about, anyway?"

"Stuff," Tor shrugged.

Tor maybe didn't say much – especially at school – but he was still a popular guy. There was always a procession of small chums from his class trampling around our house being introduced to all the pets. Maybe different things make you popular when you're older, but when you're seven, having the equivalent of Rolf's *Animal Hospital* at home works pretty well.

"What kind of stuff?" I pushed him.

Today in particular I was quite up for losing myself in Tor's world. It distracted me from what was looming in front of me ... i.e. my blind date. I was planning on keeping myself really busy until it was time to get ready, just so I wouldn't go round the twist thinking about it.

"Stuff," shrugged Tor again, taking a slurp of his drink. "I did a picture of a snail and Freddie said it looked like a big poo."

I know ('cause I remember) that when you're Tor's age, things like that matter – a *lot*. But still, if that was all he had to worry about, then I was pleased. He had plenty of time to grow up and worry about life, the universe, exams and everything.

"You and Linn and Rowan…" said Tor suddenly, fixing me with a serious stare.

I was tempted to lean over and wipe away the frothy chocolate moustache on his upper lip, but I thought he might get grumpy about me babying him.

"What? What about us?" I asked, sneaking a look at my watch. (Nine hours to go before I had to meet up with Kyra…)

"You all think Dad's got a girlfriend."

I choked so much on a mouthful of hot chocolate that it nearly sprayed out of my nose (mmm!). Frantically, I tried to think of something to say – some reassuring denial – but my mind let me down. Several pathetic explanations popped into my brain, and were so pathetic that they popped right out again.

Tor kept staring at me as his nose disappeared back into his mug.

He may be a weird kid, but he's so smart. Smarter than his three sisters put together, that was for sure. We thought we were so clever, hiding everything from him, and he saw through it all.

"He's going out with her on Sunday," said Tor matter-of-factly, wiping his mouth with the back of his hand.

It was just as well I hadn't taken another slurp of hot chocolate, or it really would have been spraying out of my nose in surprise at *that* little pronouncement. It seemed that Tor not only knew what *we* knew, he knew *more*...

"He's going out on Sunday? How do you know?" I quizzed him, giving up any pretence at denying anything. Why bother?

"I asked Dad if we could go to the City Farm on Sunday," Tor explained. "He said he couldn't, he had to do a *thing*. And he went bright red."

Look at that – my brother was even smarter than our *dad*, seeing through his excuse straight away. (Still, saying he was doing a "thing" was a pretty *pitiful* excuse on Dad's part and not *that* hard to see through, I guess.)

"Are you going to follow him this time?" Tor asked straight out.

I was slap-bang stunned. Again.

"Did you know that's what Linn and Rowan were trying to do on Wednesday night?" I asked him, remembering how his questioning had put a stop to my sisters' attempts at spying.

"Uh-huh," nodded Tor, playing around with the

fish-scoop again.

"Why didn't you tell us you knew what was going on?"

"You were leaving me out," said Tor simply.

I guess he had a point.

"Listen, we'll talk to Rowan and Linn when we get home," I told him. "And we won't leave you out again, OK?"

Tor nodded happily. I guess we thought we were protecting him, but all the time we were making him feel lonely and pushed out with our sisterly secrets.

Still, it looked like Love Child No. 4 was just about to join the family firm of private investigators.

Dad didn't stand a chance.

Chapter 14

THIS WAY FOR A SPEEDY EXIT...

Time was dragging. It had been a busy (and draining) day, but this last couple of hours before I was due to go and meet Kyra were stretching out like the world's biggest elastic band...

My day had gone like this: after my brother's little bombshell in the café, the two of us had traipsed home, rounded up Rowan (Linn was out), and filled her in on Inspector Tor's powers of deduction. What Tor had said about Sunday tied in with the suspect message Gran had given Dad the other evening, but until we could get hold of Linn, there was no point working out what to do about it.

After that, I went round to see Sandie. I was in serious grovelling mode; she'd said on the phone that she didn't mind if I blew her out for the party (and the date), but I knew she was gutted really. She'd asked me all these questions: "What's this boy like?" (I didn't know); "Where's the party?" (I didn't know); and "What are you going to wear?" (Yep, I didn't know – since none of my other friends were going, the dress-rehearsal ritual hadn't happened). And all the time, Sandie kept looking at me with her big Disney eyes all soulful and sad.

I finally escaped (from the guilt) when her mother came up to take her temperature and check she hadn't developed the *plague* or something. On the way home, it suddenly struck me that Sandie was probably worried that me and Kyra had got too buddy-buddy while she was stuck at home with her gastric-flu thing. It wasn't really like that, but I could see why she thought it might be.

But as they say, that was then and this is now. And right about now, I was standing under the shower, feeling very, very sick.

(Mind you, it's not hard to feel ill in our bathroom. Mum painted the walls deep ruby red, 'cause she wanted to put lots of plants in here, and thought the greenery would look great against it. Only it practically gives you a *migraine* if you stay in the room more than ten minutes.)

His name was Bobby, this guy I was feeling sick about. Kyra had told me that much, and that was *all* she'd told me, apart from the fact that him and Ricardo went to the same school. I guess that was as much I could expect from Kyra, considering she'd only been going out with Ricardo for a week, and probably didn't know that much about him either (apart from an intimate knowledge of his snogging technique).

So, with two hours to go, I was standing in the shower, letting the torrent of water batter over my head, and – get this – trying to think of things I could talk about with Ricardo's mate.

How pathetic was that? But you know, that was (actually, it still *is*) something I worry about a lot. A *lot*. I mean, what are you meant to speak to each other about on dates? Once you've run through all the stuff about *likes* and *dislikes*, and who your mates are and everything, I worry that you just dry up. At least, it was like that when I went out with Keith Brownlow (urgh, don't remind me...), and even though we're about a million light years away from *ever* dating, it's like that with Alfie too – my mind just goes blanker than blank when I get the chance to talk to him.

Now Billy, that's different – 'cause he's just a mate, same as Sandie, or Chloe or the others (well, with a couple of genetic differences...). I can talk to Billy for *hours* about *anything* (mostly rubbish, if you want to know, but it's always pretty entertaining rubbish).

So what happens to your brain when you fancy someone, or you're out on a date? Why does it seem like having a normal conversation is about as alien as nipping to Saturn for your summer holidays?

My eyes suddenly started stinging with shampoo, so I rammed my face under the flow of the water, and tried to distract myself from the pain by coming up with things I could talk about.

And this was all I managed...

1) Ask him what subjects he's doing at school. (Nah – it would make me sound like a total swot...)

2) Ask him what football team he's into. (What's the point? I don't know anything about football, so it would be a really *short* conversation. Him: "And what football team do you support?" Me: "Uh, none." Him: "Oh." See? Not exactly scintillating...)

3) Tell him the stories behind my brother and sisters' names. (Nope – he'll think we're all weirdos. Which isn't far off the case when it comes to Rowan...)

4) Ask him what he wants to do when he leaves school. (Sounds too heavy. He'll expect me to ask how many children he wants and if he's got a pension plan next...)

5) Tell him that I share a house with two dogs, five cats, three hamsters, too many white mice to count, a one-eyed iguana, four rabbits, a couple of

tanks of fish, a pile of stick insects, a recuperating pigeon and whatever else Tor's brought home lately. (*Definitely* not – I want him to think I'm this cool, desirable girl, not Dr Dolittle...)

It was no use.

I gave up, turned the shower off and stepped out of the bath, dripping. The water pipes to the shower shuddered to a halt, like there was a tiny man behind the wall, hammering like crazy. (Maybe there is – who knows? Or a poltergeist of an irate Victorian plumber?)

Wiping away the steam on the old, chipped, wood-framed mirror above the sink (a junk-shop treasure my mum once came home with), I checked out my reflection – and saw a big pink prawn staring back at me. I'd obviously stayed in the shower just a *little* bit too long. In fact, I was *so* pink, I clashed horribly with the red walls. I had to get out of there – get up to my room, open the windows wide, and cool down. How could I go and meet the mysterious Bobby if I looked like I'd fallen asleep under a sun-lamp?

Rifling through the towels in the cupboard, the only one I could find that was big enough to cover my bits was one of those emergency towels – an ancient, threadbare, ratty one that you keep in case the others are all in the wash, and hope you never need to drag out. But it would have to do; today was laundry day and all the half-decent towels were outside twirling on the washing line along with the clothes.

"Mmm – very sexy. *Not!*" I murmured at my dripping, pink, ratty reflection.

The old bolt on the bathroom door was as sticky as ever, and I had to give it a good tug to get it open.

Does nothing in this stupid house work properly? I moaned to myself, realizing immediately that I was starting to sound worryingly like Linn. If she had her choice, Linn's dream house would be some ultra-modern, ultra-sleek, ultra-minimalist effort like you see in those interiors magazines – not a pipe-rattling, door-sticking, madly-painted wreck like our place.

In my general stress-induced state of grumpiness, I hadn't noticed the creak on the stairs coming up from the hallway. Suddenly, I saw Alfie's scruffy blond hair coming into view, just when I was about as far away as I could be from the escape route of the stairs to the attic (which were at the other end of the landing).

Emergency! If there was one thing I was sure of, it was that I did *not* look like a moist-skinned, semi-nude goddess. I looked like I'd been *stewed*, for God's sake, and I could feel an ominous draft whistling round my bum, from what must have been a large hole in this disgrace of a towel.

Up till now, I'd had precisely zero chance of ever going out with Alfie. If he saw me like this, my chances would dip down to minus a *million*.

Thankfully, Alfie's face was turned and looking back down at Linn, who I could hear chatting behind him. This gave me a split-second's grace to vanish, before I embarrassed myself more than I'd ever been embarrassed in my life (and there were plenty of times *that* had happened, I can assure you...).

The closest door to me led into Dad's room and, quick as a pink flash, I slipped in there, shutting the door silently behind me. Sighing, I leant my whole weight against the door. (What for? In case Alfie had caught a glimpse of me and tried to barge his way in after me, unable to control his passion at the sight me in my peek-a-boo towel? I don't *think* so.)

As my heart rate began to slow down (from frantic to only marginally *less* frantic), my eyes drifted across the room. It was flooded with a cosy orange glow, partly from the early evening sunlight streaming in through the window, and partly because the walls themselves were orange (a kind of ginger-cat colour – Colin was completely camouflaged whenever he came in here for a snooze).

Outside on the landing, I could make out the mumble of conversation and the squeaky tread of stairs, as Linn and Alfie headed up to her room. I could relax... Or at least give myself a chance to cool down, and nick a pair of jogging bottoms and a T-shirt from Dad's wardrobe so that I could get back up to my room with a little more decorum.

I walked over to the wardrobe and pulled the door open. It was packed – but not all with Dad's stuff. There were loads of Mum's dresses and everything in there. All beautiful, patterned fine cottons and Indian silks, a couple of velvet jackets, and some cheesecloth tops. I knew without looking that all her favourite chunky old jumpers would be where they always were, folded up in the big bottom drawer of the chest by the bed. Dad's kept all her stuff just as she left it – perfume bottles, make-up (not that she ever wore much) and an old hairbrush all sit on the dressing table, in case she just happened to stroll through the door and want to pick up where she left off...

There are reminders of Mum all over the house – not just in the way she decorated it, but her paintings and pottery and everything are on every wall and on practically every spare surface. But this room in particular is like a mini-shrine to her, and it's nice to come in here now and again, just on those weird occasions when I feel like I'm starting to forget little things about her, and smell her perfume or pull out her favourite clothes.

And of course, there's her self-portrait right above the bed. Not that you might recognize it as a self-portrait, since it's just all a mass of swirly oranges and yellows. In case you were wondering, it represents her aura. (An aura is some spooky electric current that we all have around us, according to ... well, people who read auras. Normal people can't see them, but aura readers can; and one of them told Mum that hers symbolized "awakening". I think I go through so many feelings and moods in a day that *my* aura would be brown – like when you get all those brilliant Plasticine colours that turn to sludge when you mix them.) Anyhow, my mum came back home after getting her aura reading done at a Mind, Body and Spirit Festival at Alexandra Palace, and immediately started working on this painting. She left home on her travels about two weeks after that, so I reckon that aura reader's got a lot to answer for, if you ask me...

But back to that afternoon, when all I had on

was that awful scabby towel. Suddenly, I found myself sitting on the edge of Mum and Dad's big old squeaky wooden bed, staring at her painting and remembering the Sunday mornings when we all used to pile in – even Linn. Nowadays, Tor still dive-bombs Dad occasionally (along with Winslet and Rolf), and it's funny to see, but it's not the same as those long-ago times when all us girls and Mum were part of the fun.

I shook myself, aware that I was starting to get too sad about everything. Quickly – before the tears had a chance to get hold of me – I got to my feet and began hunting through the wardrobe, yanking an old denim shirt off a hanger and hauling it on. Some more searching, and I'd found a pair of Dad's jogging bottoms that were far too big for me but at least made me look more human and less like pond-life.

I went over to the dressing table to check out my general redness levels, when I spotted something lying open by the side of the bed.

It was a photo album – one of the ones that normally lived in the cupboard in the living room. What had Dad taken it up here for?

I flopped down on the floor and pulled it round to face me. It was open at a page of photos of Mum: Mum holding her long skirt up and paddling in the sea; Mum laughing at some unknown joke; Mum in the long, wispy lavender dress she got married in; Mum grinning by a muddy stream, wearing wellies, dungarees and stroking her round, pregnant tummy.

What had made Dad dig these out?

I glanced up again at the large framed painting hanging over the bedhead.

"Oh, Mum," I mumbled, wishing I was looking at her face for real, instead of a bunch of stupid orange and yellow swirls. "What do you think's going on? Do you think Dad's feeling guilty about something…?"

Chapter 15

BLIND DATES AND FRAYED NERVES

It was the first time I'd ever seen Kyra without her hair scraped back into her bunched-up ponytail. With her curls waxed, her mid-brown hair looked darker and glossier, pinned back from her face with coloured butterfly clips.

It suited her. You know how she's got those sort of sticky-out ears? Well you couldn't even tell they were sticky-out at all with her hair like that. Not one bit.

"I know I've said it already, but you look really nice," I told her, in a squeakier-than-normal voice.

It was a tough job keeping my frayed nerves under control. I couldn't do much about my voice, but at least I could stick my hands (which were suffering from a bad case of tremble), deep down in my trouser pockets.

"Thanks! You look pretty OK too!" she smirked, raising her eyebrows at me.

We'd just got off the bus and were heading for Ricardo's house, with Kyra holding a scruffy bit of paper with directions on it. We were now on the north side of Alexandra Palace, not a million miles away from Billy's house (I hoped we wouldn't bump into him – he'd have killed himself laughing if he'd seen how dressed up I was). Now that we were here, I realized that if I'd known how close Ricardo's house was, I'd have suggested that we just walk over the park.

But then I took a look at the black, satiny wedge sandals that Kyra had on her feet, and knew that grass, earth and those shoes would definitely *not* go...

I was just wearing a pair of trainers (but my best pair, of course). I can't wear anything with heels – they make me walk like a duck. And unlike Kyra, who was wearing a little chiffon, flowered skirt, my legs were well covered up, in my cut-off khaki trousers. Kyra had dared to bare with her top (a little black halterneck thing), but again I played safe, sticking to my favourite T-shirt: the khaki one with the red star on the chest.

It wasn't so much my clothes that would have made Billy laugh – it was my make-up. Or more like *Kyra's* make-up. When we'd met at the bus stop, she'd frowned at me, then rummaged in her bag and pulled out a little pot. Next thing, she's holding up a mirror and showing me the twinkles of glitter she's daubed on my cheeks and eyelids.

"That looks so cool on you!" Kyra had announced, and I didn't have the guts to contradict her.

A couple of lads in a car honked their horn at us as we trotted along the road, still searching for Ricardo's street. I didn't know whether it was the sight of Kyra's long brown legs that had driven the boys to hammering on their horn, or if the glitter on my face was blinding them and they were trying to let me know I was a traffic hazard.

"Is it far now?" I asked, trying to sneak a peek at the squiggles on the piece of paper Kyra was holding.

"No – this is the road here!" she announced, swinging a left into a street full of small terraced houses.

"Thanks again for inviting me," I muttered, even though at that point I felt so nervous I was pretty tempted to turn and run – very fast – all the way home.

"No problem," said Kyra, brightly. "I kind of felt sorry for you after what you were saying earlier in the week…"

Great. She hadn't fixed me up on this double date because I was smart, or funny, or interesting or pretty – she'd invited me because she felt *sorry* for me. How useless did that make me feel?

"After I was saying what exactly?" I quizzed her.

I tell you one thing: getting defensive is a good way to stop feeling nervous.

"Oh, it was when you were talking about fancying that friend of your sister's. The one you said you don't stand a chance with," said Kyra, bluntly. "So, I just thought it might cheer you up to snog Ricardo's mate."

An avalanche of nerves descended upon me again.

Oh my God. Did this guy *assume* I was going to snog him? If Kyra was sure it was going to happen, then her boyfriend must be sure too, and – naturally – his mate as well. I mean, I had no objection to the idea of kissing someone if I really liked them, but the thought that everyone expected it to be a done deal was only completely petrifying…

I didn't have any more time to think about it (or invent a sudden illness that had struck me out of the blue so I could get away *fast*) – Kyra was sashaying up to a navy-blue front door and ringing a bell.

I gulped, and just knew I'd gone pink again.

"Hi!" said a dark-haired lad, pulling the door open.

He glanced my way for a nano-second, then grinned slowly as he eyed Kyra up and down. Joey out of *Friends* had nothing on this guy.

"Hi, Ricardo!" Kyra smiled coquettishly, twirling and swaying on the doorstep. "This is Ally…"

"Yeah? I couldn't remember what you said she was called," said Ricardo, with minimum tact and charm.

Mmm, it might be a bit of a struggle to like this guy, I decided.

"Anyway, this is my mate," he continued, pointing his thumb back over his shoulder in the general direction of the hallway, where a tall, shadowy figure ambled towards the doorway.

"Hi, Bobby!" said Kyra, wafting her fingers in a wave towards Ricardo's buddy.

I took one look at Bobby and froze.

He took one look at me, and seemed like he was going to laugh or hurl – one of the two.

"His name's not Bobby," Ricardo snorted. "It's Billy!"

"Bobby … Billy," Kyra shrugged off her mistake with a cheeky air of casualness. "What's the difference?"

It's the difference, I felt like telling her, between having a proper blind date, and being set up with your own best *mate*…

Chapter 16

THAT'S *SOME* PARTY TRICK...

I glanced around the room. Yep, it was just like I suspected when we first walked in: everyone at this party seemed a *lot* older than us – fifteen or sixteen at least. I hoped I didn't look as young as I suddenly felt.

Just as I was nervously checking everyone out, I became aware of a pair of eyes staring at me, from only a few centimetres away.

"What *is* that stuff on your cheeks?" asked Billy, wrinkling his nose up as he inspected my face.

"Pure gold dust. What did you think?" I replied, sarcastically.

Some party this was shaping up to be. The whole of the flat we were in was crowded with people (i.e. boys) I'd never met, and I'd never get a *chance* to get to know any of them – not with Billy in tow. Even if a cool sixteen year old was interested in going out with someone who was only thirteen. (Like, fat chance...)

It's at times like these you suddenly appreciate

the differences between female and male friends. If I was with Sandie or Salma or someone, people would assume I was single. But standing with this lanky berk of a boy – especially when he was pawing at my face the way he was – anyone was bound to suppose we were an item.

"Gerroff!" I moaned, pushing his finger away from my eyeball.

"I just wanted to see what that stuff was!" he whined. "Is it like little bits of metal, or what?"

"It's a gel, with glitter in it," I sighed, knowing I'd better give him an answer or he'd just keep annoying me. "Kyra's got a little pot of it. Why don't you go and ask her if you can try some?"

I stared over at Kyra and Ricardo, who were busy getting to know each other better on the sofa (i.e. recreating their snogathon at the bus stop when I saw them the other night).

"Nah, I won't bother," grinned Billy. "Just looking at you, I can see that it's crap."

"Thanks!" I said, rolling my eyes.

I still hadn't quite got over the shock of finding out that Billy was my date for the night. Billy, of course, thought it was the funniest thing in the world. It turned out that Ricardo had only told him he was set up on a blind date about half an hour before me and Kyra arrived (like I said before, boys are useless when it comes to important details).

"He told me your name was Emma, or Wendy or something," Billy had told me, as we'd headed off to the party after our bizarre "introduction" on the doorstep – *and* once Kyra and Ricardo had stopped wetting themselves laughing.

"But didn't you even recognize Kyra's name when he was talking about her?" I'd asked him.

Kyra was pretty unusual (the name *and* the girl), and he'd heard me moan about her enough when she'd first started at school and got right up my nose.

"I didn't know what she was called. I just knew Richie had a new girlfriend, that's all," he'd shrugged. (See what I mean about being useless?)

And there was the other twist of the night. Ricardo wasn't an unknown quantity to me at all – Billy had mentioned him loads of times in the passing, but as Richie, not Ricardo. He wasn't a close friend of Billy's or anything, it was just that they played on the same football team. The one nugget I'd remembered hearing about "Richie" was that he was a real success with the girls. Billy was slightly in awe of his success rate in actual fact: Richie seemed to be going out with a different girl practically every week.

Which didn't exactly bode well for Kyra...

"Come on – let's dance!" said Billy, trying to drag me into the centre of the room as a hip-hop track burst on to the sound system.

"No, I'm not in the mood," I shrugged.

"Aw, Ally!" he pleaded, tugging at the bottom of my T-shirt and doing this goofy little dance in front of me, rolling his shoulders and jumping around on the spot.

"No!" I giggled, shaking free of him.

He's such an idiot, you can't help laughing at him sometimes. And the thing is, he just *looks* funny as well – like he grew too quickly and bits of him haven't caught up yet. It's like his whole body's skinny-boyish, but he's got this big, man-sized nose and these huge hands and feet.

God, I'm not selling him too well, am I? I mean, despite all that, he *is* kind of cute-looking. To be honest (and I'd never tell him this), I don't really get why he hasn't got a girlfriend yet...

"*Course* you want to dance!" Billy grinned at me, grabbing me round the waist and lifting me into the centre of the room, and into the throng of dancers.

"Billy – put me down!" I squealed, battering on his shoulders with my fists. See what I mean about goofy?

As he let me slither to the ground, I noticed

something behind him. Over by the far wall, a couple of guys were watching us. They looked like they might be about sixteen, and one of them – dressed in baggy skate gear and with spiky short dark hair – was grinning this cute grin. At *me*.

I checked again, just to make sure he wasn't looking at some gorgeous model-type girl lurking behind me. He wasn't – there was that grin again.

I decided to stop protesting and dance. I'm a pretty good dancer. I know that sounds big-headed, but there are plenty of things I'm *not* good at (and I'll be the first to say so), so when there *is* something I can do quite well, I don't think it's too awful to admit to it.

Anyhow, I figured that I might just impress Skate Boy, if he was still watching me. I'm rotten at flirting (see? *There's* a thing I can't do!), so dancing well was my best shot at getting his attention. Maybe.

Three tracks later, and I'd worked up enough courage to sneak a peek in the direction of the wall.

No Skate Boy, or his mate.

Well, that was a waste of time, I grumbled to myself.

But I can't say I wasn't surprised. And anyway, I felt kind of nervous about the whole idea, if you want to know the truth. It's like, if I didn't know what to speak to Keith Brownlow about, I sure didn't know what I'd find to speak to a really cool sixteen-year-old boy about, if he'd decided to come over and talk. Which he hadn't.

"Billy – I'm going to the loo," I yelled in his ear, above the music.

"OK!" Billy yelled back, still dancing.

I'd kind of needed to go to the loo for ages, but because I'd been on my mission to impress, I'd put it off. I wished I hadn't, though – there were already three people queuing outside the bathroom door.

To take my mind off my expanding bladder, I started to daydream about the Skate Boy. What if I caught him looking at me again? What if he asked me to dance? What if we got talking? What if he asked for my phone number? What if tonight I ended up with a date after all? But I was rushing way, way, *way* ahead of myself.

I took a long, slow, deep breath... Once I'd been to the loo, I decided, I'd trawl through the flat, and see if I could locate him in the crush of people. I might not have the courage to go right up and talk to him (like, duh!), but at least if I hung out in the same room as him it would up my chances of getting to know him. And I'd just have to worry about what to say to him when (if!) it happened...

"Ally! Oh, brilliant – you're next!"

Kyra appeared at my side, irritating everyone who'd started to queue behind me. While I'd been daydreaming, I hadn't even been aware of the fact that the three people in front of me had been and nearly gone.

"I'm absolutely desperate, Ally – can I nip in before you?" Kyra pleaded. "I'll be quick!"

"Well…" I said, dubiously, knowing I was about to get steamrollered.

"Aw, thanks!" Kyra smiled, crossing her arms across her chest and doing tiny hopping movements from side to side.

At that moment, the bathroom door opened, and practically before the poor girl had come out, Kyra was barging past, dragging me in tow.

It seemed we were to have our first girls-gossiping-in-the-loos moment.

"So how are things going with your hot date?" giggled Kyra mischievously, as she plonked herself down on the loo.

"Don't!" I moaned. "And it's all *your* fault. If you'd remembered which school Ricardo went to, and got Billy's name right in the first place, I *might* have sussed it out…"

"Whatever," yawned Kyra, in that irritating way she's got.

But that's what Kyra's like – really good fun and also kind of infuriating. But as I was getting to know her, I was slowly learning *not* to get too wound up by the infuriating side of her character.

"So?" I asked, sensing that she was probably more interested in talking about her own situation than mine. "Are you having a good time?"

In the harsh bathroom light I couldn't help noticing the vivid red rash below her bottom lip and on her chin. A telltale sign of her snogging marathon…

"Well, yeah. It's OK…" Kyra replied, scrunching up her face slightly.

"*That* doesn't sound too enthusiastic!" I frowned.

I'd expected her to be raving on about how fantastic Richie/Ricardo was. What was going on? Had something happened? Maybe Richie/Ricardo was up to his old tricks; maybe Kyra had spotted him eyeing up next week's potential girlfriend.

"Well, I've decided I'll probably chuck him," said Kyra matter-of-factly, as she stood up, smoothed her skirt back down and turned on the sink tap to wash her hands.

I knew it was my turn to go, but I was too surprised to do anything about it.

"You want to *chuck* him?" I gasped. "How come?"

"I'm kind of bored with him. He's really into football and stuff that's just dull, dull, dull…"

Kyra was gazing into the mirror above the sink, inspecting her reflection and running her finger under her eyes where her mascara had started to run.

"Are you going to chuck him *tonight*?" I asked.

I felt almost sorry for Richie/Ricardo, even if he hadn't done or said anything to make me like him. It looked like the heartbreaker was in for a bit of a shock.

"Nah. He's a good kisser. I won't chuck him till tomorrow."

Maybe I'm really dumb, but I always thought you needed to *like* someone if you were going to kiss them. But then, Kyra was pretty good at baffling me.

"I thought you needed to go?" said Kyra unemotionally, glancing over towards the loo.

"Yeah, yeah," I muttered, distractedly unbuttoning my trousers and taking my turn.

If I *was about to chuck a boy*, I thought to myself, *I think I'd be a wobbly pile of jelly*.

Kyra was being so cool it took my breath away. I wondered what had happened at her other schools. Had she been out with lots of boys? Was she always this hard-nosed about them?

"And what about you, Ally? Seen anyone you like here?" asked Kyra, fluffing her curls up with her fingers and readjusting some of her butterfly clips.

"Um, well, I saw this cute boy when I was dancing earlier…" I said, slightly shyly.

"Yeah? What's he like?" she asked, her eyes lit up at the prospect of gossip.

Before I could tell her, there was a hammering at the door.

"Hurry up! Get out of there! NOW!" came a muffled male voice, along with other mumbles from a variety of voices.

I glanced at Kyra, both of us a bit shaken at being yelled at like that, even if there was a large chunk of wood between us and the shouty lad.

Quickly, I got myself together, flushed the loo and opened the door – only to be pushed aside by two lurching boys falling into the room.

"Jeez! Too late!" growled a guy I recognized as Skate Boy's mate, just as Skate Boy hurled projectile vomit all over the bathroom floor.

And Kyra's satin wedge sandals…

Chapter 17

IT'S ALL DOWNHILL FROM HERE...

It wasn't particularly late (we'd left the party early, because it had turned out to be so rubbish), but on the road that circled round the walls of Alexandra Palace, there wasn't a car to be seen.

"Look – see that flashing red light away in the distance?" I pointed out to Kyra. "That's Canary Wharf, down in the Docklands. And that light over there? That's the Telecom Tower, in the West End."

"Wow!" said Kyra, pulling her little black cardie tighter around her body in the chilly evening air. "I'll have to bring my dad up here – he'll love it!"

"You get a better view in the day, though," Billy chipped in. "You can make out the Dome then too."

"Why didn't you point out this stuff when we came up here to the skating the other night?" Kyra chastised Richie/Ricardo.

Richie/Ricardo just shrugged.

I felt like pointing out to her that they were probably too busy snogging when they weren't actually skating at the rink. And when you've got your eyes closed and someone else's face in your way, it's hard to appreciate a view.

"And since we're sightseeing," said Billy. "You see that bench down there?"

"No," replied Kyra, peering down into the unlit, grassy expanse of the park below.

"No, neither can I," Billy, the big joker, agreed with her. "But anyway, there *is* a bench down there, and that's where me and Ally meet up every Sunday, with our dogs. Isn't it, Al?"

"Yep," I nodded, as I turned off the pavement and started walking down the steps into the darkness.

"Where are you going?" asked Kyra, sounding a little concerned.

"We're going down the hill," I told her.

The boys had offered to walk us to the other side of Ally Pally, where – back in the glare of the street lights – me and Kyra could make our separate ways home.

"What – straight down the hill?!" frowned Kyra dubiously. "But I thought we'd just follow the road around!"

"But going down the hill's much quicker," I explained.

(I was trying to convince myself as well as Kyra

at that point – I knew my dad would flip out if he knew we were cutting across the park at night; he thinks that's way too dodgy. OK, so I wouldn't do it on my own, or – like that night – if it was just me and Kyra, but since the boys were going to keep us company, and it wasn't exactly *late* late, I figured it would be fine, just this once. And I planned on sticking the money Dad had given me for a taxi back into his jeans pocket, since it's not like he's got gallons of money to chuck about.)

"And going down the hill's more fun!" grinned Billy. "Come on – run!"

And with that he grabbed my hand and pulled me after him, running headlong into the darkness, where only the tallest branches of the trees stretching up into the starry sky showed any shape.

Half-laughing, half-shrieking, I tumbled after him.

"*I'm* not running down there – it's dark! I could step in dog poo and not realize it! Why can't we just— No, Ricardo! Ricardo! *Waaaaaaahhhhhh!*"

From the thudding of running footsteps and shrieking giggles coming from Kyra, it didn't sound like Richie/Ricardo had given her a choice. They were right behind me and Billy as we crashed through the rustling, tall grass, halfway down the hill.

Mind you, I didn't know why Kyra was so bothered about the risk of getting dog poo on her precious shoes – not when they'd already been barfed on that night. Even though we'd done a good job of cleaning them up at the kitchen sink, they were still pretty much ruined...

Actually, I think it's safe to say that after the barfing incident, me and Kyra both had a change of heart about our boys. Once we'd cleaned off her shoes and made our way back to the living room (Kyra leaving a trail of wet footprints where she walked), it suddenly became blindingly obvious that practically every lad at the party – not just Skate Boy and his mate – was horribly, obnoxiously drunk. By comparison, Richie/Ricardo and Billy were reassuringly sober, and it was a relief to be back in their company.

"Where have you been?" Billy had asked me when I finally found him, now slouched on the sofa beside Richie/Ricardo. "I thought you were off trying some of that lethal cocktail stuff. I thought I was going to have to roll you home!"

The cocktail stuff that Billy had heard about was the reason so many of the lads (and loads of the girls) at the party were trashed. Billy had heard that someone had found a big bowl and was pouring *everything* alcoholic into it – whatever bottles people had brought had been chucked in there, as well as stuff that had been raided from the house.

I felt kind of sorry for the boy whose party it was – his parents were going to kill him when they saw how trashed their house was and how much of their own booze supply had been raided. But Billy told me not to waste my time: the guy whose party it was the one who was making the "cocktails"…

"Yeah, suckers – we're beating you!" Ricardo called out, streaking past us with a yelping Kyra, the two of them just hazy blurs in the darkness.

"You want a race? You've *got* a race!" Billy yelled after them. "C'mon, Al!"

I gasped breathlessly as we hurtled headlong down the hill, Billy still holding my hand tight. It was funny; I'd been building up the party in my head since I'd heard I was going, and yet this – acting like a ten year old, with my best mate – was much more fun than anything else had been the whole night. (Although, in a *weird* way, I'd quite enjoyed Skate Boy's little party trick – it was just the novelty of a boy making a fool of himself in front of *me*, instead of the other way round…)

Finally, the hill slipped away into the flat, grassy expanse at the bottom, and the occasional window light from the flats that backed on to Ally Pally lit our faces with a watery light.

"We won!" Billy panted, holding my hand aloft in the air.

Richie/Ricardo and Kyra didn't say anything – they just grinned and tried to get their breath back. But I noticed the way they were standing with their arms round each other. It looked like Kyra might have changed her mind about chucking him quite yet...

"Hey," said Richie/Ricardo, once he could speak. "You said you lived over in Palace Heights Road, didn't you?"

He was talking to me (and I suspected he still didn't remember my name).

"Yes," I nodded.

"Well," he panted, "that entrance over there is closest to you. But the entrance over there is closer to Kyra's. So we're going *that* way..."

Even in the faintly lit gloom, I could see the way that Kyra was gazing mushily into his eyes. Looked like the two of them were telling us in no uncertain terms that they were off for a romantic stroll – and we were not invited.

As we waved the two of them off, I turned to Billy.

"You don't have to come any further," I told him. "You'll just have to go all the way back up over the hill."

"Nah, it's all right," he shrugged, starting to walk down towards the alleyway. "I'm thirsty after all that running. I'll walk you down to that twenty-four-hour shop on the main road and get a Coke or something, and then maybe get the bus home."

OK, so I was doing a total turnaround. Suddenly, I remembered one of the advantages of male friends compared to female friends – they can act like your protector the way a girl can't.

We had just come out of the alleyway into a sleepy little street, when Billy came out with something that nearly squeezed what little air I had left right out of my lungs.

"Hey, I meant to say," he shrugged, his hands shoved in his jeans pockets. "What was my mum phoning your dad about the other night?"

"Huh?" I blinked at him.

Sure, my dad knew Billy's mum, but only vaguely. My own mum had been quite pally with her – they'd met when Billy and I were in playgroup together. But Dad didn't know her or Billy's dad particularly well at all. I mean, if they bumped into each other round Crouch End, then they'd stop and say hello and stuff, but calling each other up?

"What, didn't he say she'd phoned?" asked Billy.

I shook my head, silently.

"Well, maybe I got it wrong. It was just that I heard her call whoever it was 'Martin', and I just thought of your dad. It was probably some other guy she knows. She knows loads of people. She's got a better social life than *me*."

I tried to tell my befuddled head that that was the answer. She was talking to someone else, not my dad. No way.

"You know, it must have been someone else, 'cause she was arranging to meet them on Sunday. Tomorrow, I mean," Billy shrugged.

There were shivers zipping up and down my back. I didn't know what to think, what to say, what to do.

"Billy," I suddenly found myself choking out, "thanks for walking me over the hill, but I've got to run, I'm really late…"

I didn't even give Billy a chance to say bye as I pounded the pavement at top speed. I didn't even think about the fact that he must be wondering what I was on about (late? How could I be late when we'd ducked out of the party early?). All that was in my head was the memory of Gran passing that message on to Dad on Thursday.

"If you're still up for Sunday, then give her a call," I muttered, repeating the message as I ran, my heart pounding.

Call "her".

Billy's mum.

I just couldn't believe it…

Chapter 18

IT CAN ONLY GET WORSE...

I stared at the map on the wall, faintly lit by the light from the street lamp outside my window, since I'd left my curtains open.

I felt restless and hot under the covers, and kicked my duvet off me.

An indignant "Prrrp!" from the bottom of the bed made me realize that a small, furry entity had been adding to the temperature of my overheating bed.

"Sorry," I whispered, to a cat that wasn't Colin, as I sat upright and hauled the duvet off it.

Before I could identify which cat it was, it thumped off the bed in a grump, heading off to another part of the room where its sleep wouldn't be so rudely disturbed.

Now that I was sitting, I let my hand stretch up the wall and touch the jutting-out coloured pins that mark all the places Mum has sent letters home from. Sometimes the pattern of the pins confuses me; they seem so random, like she's doubling back on herself a lot of the time. One time, she'll be in

Thailand, then a couple of months later we'll get a letter from America, then it'll be back to Indonesia again. "How can she afford it?" I asked Linn once, when I was old enough to work out that travel wasn't free. "All the long-term backpackers know how to live on next to no money," she'd told me, like she knew the answer to everything (which she usually does). "They all tell each other where the cheapest places are to stay, or where they can go and work for a while. And look what Mum's said when she's written – she's painting T-shirts and selling them, or waitressing sometimes too. That's how she pays for travelling."

What was most annoying was that she was on the move so much, she never had an address long enough for us to write back to her. That was hard, only having this one-way contact with her. There'd been plenty of times when I really, really felt that I needed to talk to her. Like now...

But what could I possibly write? "Dear Mum – remember your friend Sharon? Billy's mum? Well, it looks like she's having an affair with Dad..."

I shuddered at the thought and felt suddenly cold. Gathering up the duvet, I bundled myself up against the headboard, and – with only my nose sticking out – I stared off out of my window at the faraway outline of Alexandra Palace.

I mean, Billy's mum, of all people! She's *so* not like my mum. She's this neat-freak with a house full of stuff that's so new it's practically still got the price tags on. She runs some clothes section in a department store in Wood Green. The kind of clothes she sells, they're all sort of *womanly* and *middle-aged*, if you see what I mean. You know – jackets with gold buttons and knee-length skirts, worn with smart, high-heeled shoes. I know she's got to dress like that at work, but she dresses like that at home too. I think if I ever went round to Billy's and saw her in a pair of jeans and without her hair blow-dried, I'd faint.

I know I might sound like I'm judging by appearances (guilty!), but there's another thing about Billy's mum – she orders people about in that patronizing management way in the store, and does *that* at home too. "Billy," she'll say, lifting his feet off the coffee table, "we have standards!"

I don't know how Billy's dad stands it. (Not that I know Billy's dad too well even after all these years; he's one of those people who looks at children and teenagers like they're an unknown species, as if he's never been one himself and has no idea how to communicate with them.) Billy says his dad just agrees with everything his mum says and keeps his head down in his newspaper or whatever.

Well, he might not have to do that much longer ... not if his wife's running off with my dad! I thought gloomily, feeling a sorry-for-myself pool of tears forming in my eyes.

A thump on the bed heralded the return of a cat that wasn't Colin. Tor always says that animals can sense your emotions (I don't know if that goes for stick insects too), and that they'll come to you when you need comfort. I reached my hand out from my duvet cocoon, and stroked the purry furrball – and when I felt the short stump of tail, I knew it was Fluffy.

"Hey, puss – what's going to happen, eh?" I whispered.

Fluffy rubbed her face against my nose in response.

"What if she tries to move in here?" I muttered. "She'll want to paint everything – she'll want to throw all our furniture in a skip. She'll want to get rid of loads of our animals, just so she doesn't get pet hairs on her precious business suits!"

I jolted as soon as I'd said it.

Precious.

She'd want to take her horrible, yappy, mani-cured poodle to live with us, while Rolf and Winslet would be relegated to a hut in the garden, or worse.

Then another thought struck me.

Billy – Billy would be my half-brother!

I flopped back in the bed and flung the duvet over my face.

It was all too weird and it was making my head go positively twisty...

Chapter 19

ACTION STATIONS!

If it was twisty before, my head was totally muzzy when I woke up.

There was too much noise and barking and voices and sounds blaring from the TV and the radio for this early in the morning. I forced one eye open and looked at my alarm clock – and got a shock when I saw it was half-eleven already.

I felt a dead weight on my legs and peered down the bed, to see that Fluffy had transformed into Colin at some point. He snuffled in his sleep, as I pulled my feet out from under him and swung them off the bed.

Dad and everyone must have thought I wanted a long lie-in this morning, since I was partying last night, I decided, as I pulled an old cardie over my PJs and headed for the door.

Dad had been snoring in an armchair in the living room when I got in the night before – the house was still and quiet apart from the tappity-tap of Rolf and Winslet sleepily padding over the wooden floors to investigate who'd just got in. But it wasn't the party that had tired me out and let the morning slip by – it was the fact that my brain was working overtime and hadn't shut down till who knows what time in the early hours of the morning.

"Morning, Ally – or should I say afternoon?"

I blinked down the stairs and saw Grandma gazing up at me from the hall. She was helping Tor into his jacket. Tor, meanwhile, was swapping a packet of Wotsits from one hand to the other, while trying to keep them out of Winslet's reach. So *that* was what all the barking was about.

"Hi, Grandma," I replied, rubbing my eyes and stepping down the stairs. "What are you doing here?"

"Me and Tor are going to the City Farm, aren't we?" she said, turning back to my little brother.

" 'Cause Dad can't take him..." I muttered, remembering what Tor had told me over our hot chocolate the day before.

"That's right – he's busy today," said Grandma, giving me what looked like a hint of a meaningful stare.

"Busy," said Tor, giving me a *big* meaningful stare.

I suddenly felt wide awake. I had to talk to my sisters – Linn in particular – to find what our plan of action was.

"Is Dad still here?" I asked Grandma, at the same

time nicking a Wotsit out of Tor's upheld bag, now that I was standing beside him.

"Yes. He's in the shower, I think. Right then, Tor – are we ready?"

"Uh-huh," nodded Tor, heading for the door.

"Have fun. Bye!" I called out, as I padded off towards the kitchen.

"Ally…!"

I turned and saw Tor at the opened front door, holding his thumb up to me.

That was "good luck" in code, if I wasn't very much mistaken. I nodded and put my thumb up in return.

"At last!" said Linn, looking up from the Sunday supplement she had open on the kitchen table in front of her. "Even Rowan's beaten you to it this morning."

That was amazing. Rowan was always the last to emerge from her bed at weekends. But there she was, sitting in her tartan, flannelette pyjamas, looking only three-quarters still asleep.

"Sit down, Al," Linn practically ordered me. "We haven't a lot of time. Dad's going out in half an hour. Says he's going to help 'Jake' fix his bike this afternoon!"

Linn's voice dripped with disbelief at Dad's lame excuse.

Before I did sit down, I stepped back to the kitchen door and pushed it closed. Then I walked over to the radio and turned it up louder – there was no way I wanted Dad earwigging on *this* conversation.

"Has Rowan told you what Tor heard?" I asked Linn, who was fully dressed in a black top, black jeans and trainers. Me and Rowan must have looked like bag ladies beside her...

"Yeah, she told me last night. I just wish you hadn't slept in when we needed to talk about this!" said Linn, a little snappily.

The longer I hadn't come down, the more up-tight she'd been getting, by the looks of it.

"Listen," I began, ignoring her snippy tone. "You're not going to believe what Billy said to me last night!"

"What?" asked Rowan, pushing her unruly hair back off her face.

"He said..." I paused, checking in my head that I hadn't dreamt the whole horrible thing, "that his mum had been on the phone to Dad – arranging to meet up with him today!"

Linn and Rowan stared at me with similar open-mouthed expressions. For once, they actually looked alike.

"Your mate *Billy*? His *mum* and our *dad*?" Linn repeated, incredulously.

Both of them knew who she was. At least, they knew her to say hello to, if nothing much more than that.

"Billy's mum?" squeaked Rowan, her brown eyes the size of saucers. "But isn't she married? To Billy's dad, I mean?"

"Well, *yes*," I said, rolling my eyes at her.

"What's Billy saying about it? Was he freaking out?" asked Linn, almost managing to slip back into her organized and in-control self after the shock.

Still, her skin looked paler than pale against her almost-blonde hair.

"No! He didn't get the significance – and I didn't really want to spell it out for him," I told her.

"What did he say exactly?" asked Rowan.

"Just what I said. Literally, just that he overheard her talking to 'Martin', saying she'd meet him on Sunday."

"Ally – quick, before Dad gets downstairs," said Linn urgently. "Phone Billy; ask him if he heard where they were supposed to be going!"

"If he heard it, he won't remember!" I protested. "He's a boy! Boys don't remember details!"

"Ally, you've got to try!" Linn flashed her eyes icily at me. "It's going to be really hard trying to follow Dad if we don't know where he's going, but if Billy *has* overheard something, it'll make it much easier!"

I sighed – there was no saying no to Linn.

"I'll try," I promised, pushing my chair back and heading for the hall. "But don't get your hopes up. It *is* Billy we're talking about after all…"

"Just do it," said Linn firmly.

Peering up the stairs, I could hear Dad still singing in the bathroom, while the taps in the sink rushed and the pipes gurgled and rattled.

Quickly, I dialled Billy's number.

"Hello?" came his familiar voice, after a couple of rings.

"Billy? It's me," I told him.

"Oh, hi, Al! I was just heading off for the park. Aren't you coming?"

"Uh, I hadn't thought about it," I replied, slightly flummoxed.

My brain was too fried to deal with ordinary, run-of-the-mill habits. But he'd pricked my conscience – I gazed around me in the hall, and saw two expectant doggy faces gazing back up. Rolf even had his Frisbee in his mouth.

"What are you phoning for, then?" asked Billy. "Are you OK? Did you get home all right last night? You ran off pretty fast. I thought—"

"Billy," I interrupted him, lowering my voice to a whisper, even though the singing and pipe-rattling showed that Dad wasn't about to walk out of the bathroom on me. "I need to ask you a question."

"Fire away," he said, sounding intrigued. "But why are you whispering?"

"It doesn't matter – just listen," I snapped at him, Linn-style. "Is your mum still there?"

"Uh ... no. She's just gone out. About five minutes ago."

And Dad was leaving soon too. Urgh, the whole mess *had* to be true...

"Billy, this is going to sound weird, OK, but when you heard your mum on the phone the other day – you know, when she was speaking to my dad or whichever Martin she was talking to – did you hear her say *where* she was meeting him on Sunday? Today, I mean?"

"Uh ... I don't remember."

Wow, what a surprise.

"Are you sure?" I pushed him.

"Hold on!" he said, brightly. "Dad's just through in the living room. He might know. Wait and I'll ask—"

"No!" I yelped down the phone.

It was complicated enough trying to work out what was going on with Dad and Billy's mum – we didn't need to alert Billy's dad to the fact that his wife might be cheating on him. Well, not *quite* yet...

"Why not? What's up?"

Any other day, I might have been able to come up with a sharp excuse (i.e. white lie) to cover my tracks, but since my brain was as scrambled as the eggs going cold and rubbery on Tor's plate through in the kitchen, I failed miserably.

"Billy, can you come round here? Now?"

"Why?"

"Just come, will you?"

"Um, OK. I'll be there in about half an hour. I'll take Precious with me…"

"No!" I yelped again.

My wide-awake nightmares came flooding back; I didn't want Precious coming here, trying to get his horrid little paws under the table.

"Why not?" asked Billy, sounding confused.

"Just come, will you? And quick – come on your bike?"

"Why?"

The singing suddenly stopped, and the pipes were gurgling to a halt. Dad was going to pull that door open at any second.

"See you in ten minutes!" I hissed down the phone, before slamming it back on the receiver.

Rolf nuzzled his damp nose under my hand and whined.

"I feel like that myself today," I muttered, ruffling the spiky fur on his head.

Chapter 20

I SPY WITH MY LITTLE EYE...

I don't know if Dad thought it was weird or anything, the fact that the four of us were all hovering about down at the end of the garden, but there wasn't much else we could do. The trouble was, he was wandering up and down the house too much, getting ready to go out, and the garden was just about the only place we could talk without risking him overhearing.

"*My* mum and *your* dad!" Billy exclaimed for the fortieth time since I'd told him what we suspected.

He'd taken it better than I thought he would, but to tell you the truth, I don't think it had sunk in. He had this stunned-yet-dumb expression on his face, like he'd just heard that Lara Croft had come to life and moved into the house across the road from him.

Me, I was feeling marginally calmer after my middle-of-the-night flip-out, but only marginally. I mean, I still felt really down about it all, but not so *frantic*. I know it's the sort of thing Grandma comes out with, but that stuff about "things always look better in the morning" is true, kind of. I maybe still felt totally weird about my dad being up to something with Billy's mum, but at least I'd got over that *ridiculous* idea of Billy being my half-brother. I mean, *as if*!

(Oh, please, please, *please*, God, don't let it come true!)

"Billy, are you *sure* you didn't hear where your mum was supposed to be going today?" Linn tried him again.

She was perched on the old swing, while the rest of us (and both the dogs) were hunkered down on the grass. Even at a time like this, it was pretty funny to see that Linn was still making sure her clothes stayed clean and free of grass blades.

"Nope, that's all I heard her say on the phone." He shook his head.

"Damn!" hissed Linn. "I suppose I'm just going to have to follow him when he leaves, and hope I don't lose him…"

"I'm sorry," shrugged Billy, petting Winslet, who'd moseyed up beside him and flopped her head in his lap.

"Hold on, Linnhe – how come you're saying '*I'm* going to follow him'?" Rowan demanded, peering at our sister through the pink, hexagonal sunglasses she'd shoved on to come outside. "Why should *you* go? Why don't we *all* go?"

Rowan had a point. But I had a better one.

"If anyone goes, it should be me and Billy – since *his* mum's involved in all this…"

"Rowan," said Linn flatly, completely ignoring the fact that I'd spoken. "For a start, you couldn't spy on anyone – they'd spot you a mile off."

Rowan opened her mouth to protest, then shut it again, with a slight wobble of her lip.

Linn was right, of course, and even Rowan could see that. Our in-between sister didn't know the meaning of dressing down, and no matter how well she hid, it would be practically impossible for Dad not to see a *glint* of something to do with Rowan, out of the corner of his eye.

"And *you* two," Linn continued, turning to me and Billy. "Well, OK, I see your point, but I'm coming as well."

Aha! She *had* heard me after all. And now She Who Must Be Obeyed had spoken, so it looked like the three of us had better get our spy-heads on…

"Winslet! Leave Billy alone!" I said, suddenly noticing that our small, hairy monster was showing her terrier side and trying to bury her way into Billy's jacket pocket.

"It's OK," Billy grinned, trying to gently remove her frantically snuffling nose from the inside of his jacket. But it didn't do any good. "I must have a couple of doggy biscuits left over in there from walking Precious."

There was nothing for it but forcible removal. I grabbed Winslet round the tummy and lifted her off her feet and out of Billy's pocket.

"Ewwwww! What's she eating?" cringed Rowan.

I turned her round to face me and heard the crunch of doggy treats. The trouble was, Winslet hadn't been very selective about what exactly was in Billy's pocket and also seemed to be chewing on an old snotty hankie and a piece of green notepaper.

Time for Tor's trick: I plopped her down on the grass and grabbed her by the scruff of the neck. And *voila*, her jaws flipped open and out tumbled the remains of her snack.

Winslet let out a long, low growl of irritation.

"Sorry, Billy," I apologized, picking up the piece of scrawled-on green paper by the least-chewed side. "Is this important?"

"Nah, I can't even remember what it is," he replied, flipping it round from one side to the other. "Oh, yes I can – it was just the name of this new Dreamcast game Richie phoned me up to tell me about. That's all. It's noth ... oh."

"Oh?" I repeated, watching as Billy squinted at the writing on the other side of the note.

"'The Chesterton Hotel, W1. Sun. 1 p.m.,'" Billy read out in a monotoned mumble. "Hey, this is my mum's handwriting!"

"Bingo!" I cried out, feeling my heart leap at our unexpected breakthrough.

"Really?" said Linn, out of the blue, her eyes ridiculously wide. "Hey, sounds like a good party!"

Me, Billy and Rowan stared at her. Had the sun gone to her head?

Then it clicked – we were talking in code. Dad must be in the area.

I turned around, shielding my eyes with my hand.

"Hi Dad!" I chirped, hoping I sounded cheerful (and innocent).

"Hi guys!" said Dad, wandering over in his normal weekend jeans, T-shirt and old denim jacket.

If he hadn't have slicked his hair back with gel or whatever, he wouldn't have looked at all suspicious.

"So what are you lot up to?" he asked, gazing around at all four of us.

"Oh, just hanging out. Talking about the party Ally and Billy were at last night," said Linn, very convincingly. (Give the girl an Oscar!)

"Good, was it?" he smiled down at me and Billy in particular.

"Hu-unghh…" Billy croaked, obviously too fazed by the situation to communicate in English.

"Yes!" I answered brightly, to make up for him.

"Great stuff!" nodded Dad. "Well, I better be going. Um, see you later, guys…"

"Have fun fixing Jake's bike!" Linn couldn't resist calling after him, as he strolled back to the kitchen door.

"Linn!" I hissed, once Dad was safely inside. "That sounded really sarcastic!"

"No, it didn't – you're just paranoid," said Linn, pushing herself off the swing. "Right, as soon as Dad's gone, I'm going to have to make a quick call to Alfie and blow him out – I was supposed to meet him this afternoon. Rowan, like I said, you can't come. But make yourself useful and look up the address of that hotel in the Yellow Pages. OK?"

"Uh-huh," nodded Rowan, looking none too excited by her role in the action.

"Come on, Billy," I said, standing up and hauling my brain-numbed friend to his feet. "Operation Parent-catcher starts here."

Billy blinked at me for a second, then turned the collar of his jacket up and the brim of his baseball cap down.

"Ready for action!" he saluted me.

"Billy," I sighed, "you look more like a failed member of a boy band than a spy."

I yanked the brim of his hat down till it covered his whole face…

THE FOUR MUSKETEERS...

"How much longer do you think we'll have to wait?" Billy whinged.

"For as long as it takes till they both come out," Linn said, her voice tinged with irritation.

Billy was drumming one knee up and down so fast under the table that our nearly empty cups and saucers were rattling gently on the formica table. I knew that was going to drive Linn insane (it was bugging me too, but Linn's levels of irritation are *infinitely* more finely tuned than mine...).

I stuck my hand across and grabbed Billy's knee – then pushed down hard.

"What?" asked Billy, his eyebrows knitted in confusion.

"Quit it," I told him, eyeballing him hard and trying to communicate to him through my stare that he was testing Linn's patience.

Billy scrunched up his face into an expression that said "Huh?"

Subtlety goes right over boys' heads, doesn't it?

"You're drumming your leg. It's annoying. Stop it," I spelt out for him more graphically.

Billy flopped his elbows on the table and rested his chin on his hands in real hangdog mode, but I didn't have the energy to talk him round. My nerves were ... well, all the things nerves *are* rolled into one. You name it and they were doing it: straining, fraying and jangling. And the pathetic thing was, it wasn't just the tense waiting game that was causing it, it was all because we had an extra spy in tow...

When Linn had phoned Alfie and told him she couldn't hang out with him that afternoon and why, he'd only gone and decided to invite himself along. It was a bit of a cheek really – as if he was joining us on some excellent adventure, instead of trying to find out something that could have pretty far-reaching implications on both our families and futures.

Well, that's what I'd have thought of any *other* person muscling in our spying mission, but we *were* talking Alfie, here. And I know I've got the invisible version of Rowan's rose-tinted sun-specs on when it comes to him, but what can a girl do? When your heart goes ping! your heart goes ping...

"What time is it anyway?" I asked, glancing round the café for any sign of a clock.

My heart skipped a beat or three as I spotted Alfie's messy blond hair over by the counter, where he'd gone to buy us more refills.

"Coming up for three o'clock," Linn muttered, staring down at the watch on her wrist.

We'd been sitting in the café, which (lucky or what?) was right across from the entrance to the Chesterton Hotel. By the time we'd got into town (the Tube seems to run in slow motion on Sundays), it was just after one o'clock. We weren't too bothered about missing seeing either Dad or Billy's mum heading into the hotel: as long as we knew they were there, we were happy to wait. (OK – bad choice of words: we were *willing* to wait...)

There was one little problem, though – a small niggle that kept pulsating through my mind. I wanted to say it out loud, but I was a bit scared. Scared of Linn *growling* at me over it.

Still, time was ticking away. For one thing, I had to say it out loud now, before Alfie came back to the table and I turned back into the burbling birdbrain I always was in front of him. (Luckily, both the bus and the Tube we'd taken into town were crowded, and Billy and I had had to sit at a safe distance away from Alfie and Linn. Safe, because I was far enough away not to open my mouth and say something stupid in Alfie's hearing, but not so far away that I couldn't ogle him from time to time...)

The second reason I had to make my point was that Dad and Billy's mum could come out of the hotel at *any* moment. Therefore...

"Um, Linn...?"

"What?" said Linn, staring intently over at the entrance to the hotel.

"Linn – if, I mean *when* Dad and Billy's mum come out," I began, sheepishly, "what are we ... well, what are we going to do?"

"Video them and send it in to *You've Been Framed*?" Billy jumped in, before Linn could say anything.

(I blamed mild hysteria for his bad joke. But then *all* Billy's jokes are pretty bad...)

Linn was frowning. I wasn't sure whether it was Billy being frivolous that had irked her, or me daring to question her authority (i.e. ask awkward questions). But I had a feeling I was about to find out.

But before Linn opened her mouth, someone else spoke.

"I just think you guys should play it cool..." Alfie's voice drifted down, as he hovered by my side with the tray of drinks.

I couldn't look up at him – I was frozen to the spot. I'd never, ever been this close to him before. My heart did a backflip as he leant right across me – the heat of his breath brushing my face – passing a coffee over to Linn.

"How do we play it cool?" asked Billy. "Do we say 'Hi, there! So you two are having an affair? Hey – no problem!' "

Linn flashed her eyes at Billy for daring to take the mickey out of whatever Alfie had said.

"No – I just mean, don't go out there yelling or something," Alfie drawled in his lazy, laid-back voice.

I went cross-eyed staring at his lightly tanned arm as it passed dangerously close to my nose. As he dumped a can of Lilt in front of Billy, I turned into Winslet and sniffed the air manically, trying to breathe a bit of Alfie in.

"Like, if I was you, I'd just walk along the opposite side of the pavement, saying nothing, till they saw me. Then let *them* do the talking..." Alfie continued, putting a steamy cup down in front of me. "Hot chocolate, wasn't it, Ally?"

I had to respond. I would look like a total twerp if I didn't – I'd already sat for two hours at this table letting everyone else do the talking so I didn't have to make a fool of myself.

"Cue!" I squawked.

(Translation: "Thank you!")

I turned and focussed my eyes on his face, only centimetres from my own. Those bony, high cheekbones, that long, thin nose, those pale, pale grey eyes ("same colour as a collie dog's!" Tor had so kindly pointed out once), those lips...

Er, rewind to the pale grey eyes. Where exactly were they staring right at this minute?

Only at my hand, the one that was still clutching Billy's knee next to me.

And – once again – I'd managed to make the one boy I'd *always* fancied think I was going out with the one boy I'd *never* fancy...

Chapter 22

WATCHING AND WAITING. AND WAITING SOME MORE...

"What time is it now?" I asked Linn.

"Nearly four," she mumbled, without dragging her gaze away from the entrance to the Chesterton.

She'd got into the habit of checking her watch every few minutes like a reflex action, and was probably counting every second in time with her heartbeat.

"*Yeahhhh!*" came a loud roar from the back of the café.

Linn narrowed her eyes and shot a dark look at the two boys playing on the fruit machine.

It had seemed really considerate of Alfie to suggest a turn on the machine to Billy, when Billy had begun to look a bit maudlin earlier and started mumbling stuff about his "poor dad". But half an hour later, and it looked like they were enjoying their game just that little bit *too* much; like they'd somehow managed to forget the whole purpose of our "jaunt" today...

"Boys…" tutted Linn, folding her arms across her chest. "They've got the attention span of a *newt*."

"Yep," I agreed with her.

Although, to be honest, I was kind of glad they'd moved away. I hadn't been able to look at, never mind *talk* in front of Alfie since he'd clocked me clutching Billy's knee.

"You don't think Dad and Billy's mum have left already, do you?" I asked my all-knowing sister, while systematically tearing apart the plastic cup I'd just drunk my Coke out of. (The café owners must have been toying with giving us *shares* in the place, the amount of time and money we'd spent in there.)

"Left? How could they have left?" said Linn, sounding a little short with me. "We've been sitting here watching that entrance for nearly three solid hours. Well, at least *you* and *me* have…"

"I know," I tried to agree with her. "But maybe they snuck out the back entrance or something. You know, just in case they were spotted!"

"For one thing," sighed Linn, "they aren't *expecting* to be followed, so there's no *point* in them sneaking out the back. For another, they wouldn't *go* sneaking out the back because they're not *film stars*, for God's sake. It's only *famous* people who sneak out through the kitchens – or hadn't you noticed?"

Forgive me for having such a lowly brain compared to yours, Miss Smart Alec! I felt like saying.

Except I didn't.

"Hey, I was thinking," I said instead, while eyeing up the phone box on the other side of the road, just along from the entrance to the Chesterton. "Rowan'll be at home going crazy – we should let her know what's going on."

Or *not* going on. Watching a Sunday afternoon's worth of traffic zip by was about as interesting as it had got.

"Yeah, good idea," nodded Linn.

The tension was starting to show on her, I noticed. It wasn't just her excessive snappiness (a couple of degrees up on her *normal* snappiness), it was also the fact that a couple of tendrils of hair had escaped from her scraped-back ponytail, and she *hadn't bothered fixing them*.

I rest my case.

"I've got some change. I'll go and call her from over there," I pointed to the phone box opposite.

"OK," said Linn, sounding weary.

It was all getting to her, it really was. Linn does such a good job of hiding all her emotions away (apart from the grumpy ones) that I think the very *effort* of doing that tires her out more than the rest of us.

I glanced back into the café as I made my way out of the door, and saw Billy staring intently at the display on the fruit machine while he hammered away on the buttons. At the same time, Alfie was cheering him on, grinning his wide grin and showing off that twinkling, gold back tooth.

I felt my knees buckle…

But my knees had to behave themselves once I got out in the fresh air (or traffic-polluted air, since we were in the West End of London). I had to make it across the road and into the phone box quickly, just in case Dad appeared at the front door of the hotel at that moment. I didn't really fancy getting stuck in the middle of the road and confronting him with "What exactly do you think you're doing, Dad?" while a stream of black cabs thundered in front of me, drowning me out.

Once I was safely (and breathlessly) in the phone box, I dialled our home number, then turned to stare back at the now-nearby hotel entrance while I waited for Rowan to pick up.

"Hello?" I heard her say.

"Ro?" I panted. "It's me. Listen—"

"No, hold on, Ally – I'm so glad you phoned! I've got some news…" she interrupted me.

As she began to tell me her news, I stopped staring off into the distance. Instead, I just saw my own reflection in the glass panels on the phone-box door. And all over my face was written "Oh. My. God."

The pips sounded – my twenty pence had run out. But it didn't matter; I'd heard all I needed to hear.

I replaced the handset and pushed the door open. But instead of crossing the road straight away, I made my way along the pavement to the entrance of the hotel. Right before I walked up the few marble steps that would take me into the foyer, I glanced across at the café, and saw Linn sitting where I'd left her, in the window seat, frowning over at me and mouthing "What are you doing?"

"Hold on!" I mouthed back, holding up my hand to her.

I didn't need to go all the way in to see what I needed to see. From out here on the top step, I could peer through the glass double doors at the noticeboard standing just inside. The noticeboard that had all the details of what was going on the hotel's various function suites.

"So it's true!" I heard myself say out (very) loud, as my eyes fixed on what Rowan had told me to look for…

Chapter 23

DAD'S DARK SECRET (AHEM)

"Wow. I mean, *wow*!"

It was all Sandie had been able to say since we'd filled her in on the whole sordid story. (Not, thankfully, that there was anything too sordid about it in the end...)

Sandie was sitting on the swing next to Kyra's, wrapped up (by her mother) in a padded black coat that looked a bit like a duvet. She must have been sweltering – it was a warmish Sunday evening and the rest of us weren't even wearing jackets.

"So you and Billy spent three hours sitting in some café this afternoon for *nothing*?" said Kyra, a hint of a teasing smile on her face.

I was mildly tempted to run over and shove her off the swing that she was twirling on, but I couldn't be bothered untangling my crossed legs and getting up off the ground. Also, it seemed a bit mean, since I was feeling practically giddy with relief right now.

"Well, it wasn't exactly for *nothing*, was it?" said

Billy, perched on the saddle of his mountain bike and leaning on the handlebars. "I mean, we had to try and find out what was going on, or *if* anything was going on!"

"But like you say, there *wasn't* anything going on – well, not what *you* two thought, anyway!" Kyra laughed, leaning her head languidly against one of the swing chains.

During the last couple of weeks of the Dad Drama, I hadn't breathed a word about it to Kyra. In fact, I hadn't told any of my friends except Sandie (because she's good at being super-sympathetic) and Billy (because I *had* to), and that's the way I thought it would stay. But as soon as we'd arrived at the park this evening, Billy had blabbed it all to Kyra – by accident.

What had happened was that me and Billy had arranged to meet up with Sandie in Priory Park at seven o'clock. (Billy had stayed at mine for his tea – well, after dragging him into a drama that was, after all, *not* a drama, asking him to stay for tea was the least I could do. And Rowan wasn't cooking, so it was safe.)

I was desperate to tell Sandie what we'd found out that afternoon, and Sandie was desperate to get out of the house and away from her pink cell, so the kids' playground – mercifully free of small, shrill children at that time in the evening – was where we'd decided on to meet up and catch up.

What we *hadn't* expected when we got there was to find Kyra dangling on a swing, waiting to meet Richie/Ricardo (who obviously wasn't quite dumped yet). And what *I* personally hadn't expected was for Billy to suddenly launch into a blow-by-blow account of everything that had happened that day, which was supposed to be for Sandie's ears only. I guess with the business of the party and everything, he'd just figured (wrongly) that me and Kyra were a couple of stages further along the friendship trail than we actually were. But you could tell he was regretting it now; he wasn't as used to Kyra's cheekily sarky ways as me and Sandie.

"Where's your boyfriend? Isn't he late?" I said to Kyra, changing the subject. "Maybe you got it wrong – maybe he meant for you to meet him at the kids' playground up at Ally Pally instead. That would be closer to his house…"

"Nice try, but you're not getting rid of me that easily!" grinned Kyra, seeing through my feeble attempt to distract her. "I'm enjoying hearing all this stuff far too much!"

Actually, I didn't particularly mind her teasing.

After the stresses of the last little while, it was kind of nice to have a laugh about it.

"Awww!" sighed Sandie, out of the blue, a soppy little smile on her face.

"Awww, what?" I frowned at her, wondering what planet she was currently residing on.

"I was just thinking about Tor – it's so sweet that he sorted out this whole mystery!"

You know how I said she can turn on the water-works really easily? Well, right then, it looked like she was in danger of going all gushy over my little brother. Her eyes were looking suspiciously dewy. (But then she *had* been ill with gastric flu all week. Maybe she was just suffering from a case of conjunctivitus.)

"Fnar!" snorted Kyra. "That's the funniest thing about all this, Ally! While you and your sisters all managed to convince yourselves that your dad was up to no good, a blimmin' *seven* year old is busy sussing out what's *really* going on!"

"Thanks, Kyra. Rub it in, why don't you!" I grinned back at her.

But she was right. It did seem ridiculous when you looked at it that way. After all, while me, Billy, Linn and Alfie had spent our Sunday afternoon acting like the cast of *Scooby Doo* (er, minus Scooby Doo) on the trail of skullduggery, Tor had got to the bottom of the mystery in one easy step: by asking the right person a straightforward question.

"Dad's acting weird," Tor had begun, as he and Grandma sat on the bus on the way to the City Farm. "Do you know why?"

And, as I should have expected, she did. Not much gets past our gran, whether it's something to do with us kids, or her grown-up son-in-law.

"So did your grandma know all along?" asked Sandie, so entranced with the whole story that Kyra's sarcasm was shooting over the top of her head.

"No," I replied, stretching my legs out in front of me. They were going to sleep the way I was sitting. "Like I said, she'd had her suspicions that something was going on, but it was only after she took that message for him – the one from Billy's mum – that she asked him what was up."

And here's what *was* up.

Billy's mum had no intention of getting her perfectly manicured claws into my dad (phew). Instead, it turned out she was trying to do the Girl Guide thing and do a good deed: she'd bumped into my dad on the Broadway one day a couple of weeks back, and started giving him a hard time about never getting out and having no social life (ever since Mum had gone, natch). Dad had wittered on about being happy to stay at home with us lot (bless him), but Billy's mum kept on at him. Finally, she persuaded (i.e. bullied) him to come along to the regular Wednesday evening class she and Billy's dad did.

What could Dad do? He's so easy-going, he'd never be able to say no to someone as determined and persistent as Billy's mum. And so, he found himself – wait for it…

Line dancing.

I know. Shocking, isn't it?

"No wonder your dad didn't want to tell you what he was doing!" sniggered Kyra. "I mean, *line* dancing, for God's sake! How corny is that?"

Exactly. That is *exactly* why he hadn't told us what he was up to. He said as much when we spoke to him about it this afternoon, when he'd arrived back home and seen from all our expressions that We Knew.

(Me, Linn and the boys had beaten him back to the house. After Rowan told me over the phone what was going on – Grandma and Tor had filled *her* in after they got back from their day out – I'd double-checked by reading the board in the hotel lobby. As soon as I saw "Ambassador Ballroom: Line dancing workshop, 1–5 p.m.", I'd run across the road, spilt my news, and we'd all beaten a hasty retreat back to Crouch End.)

"So you know, then?" Dad had said sheepishly, confronted by us all in the kitchen.

(By the way, we just let him believe we'd heard about his heel-toe-tapping adventures from Grandma. Admitting that we'd been trailing him halfway across London was just too sad and pathetic, and was one of those times that a white lie comes in very useful.)

"But, Dad, *line* dancing?!" I'd squeaked, incredulously.

"I know, I *know*. I don't even like country and western music!" Dad had laughed, his cheeks pink. "That's why I didn't tell you all. It was too embarrassing. And I kind of thought I'd go just the once to pacify Sharon – oh, no offence to your mum, Billy!"

"No problem!" Billy had said brightly, glad that his mother didn't have an illicit lover after all – only a stupid hobby.

"But then…" Dad shrugged and paused.

"Then what?" Linn had pushed him impatiently.

"I realized – and don't hate me for this – I *quite* enjoyed it."

None of us had a go at him for such a shameful confession. (Although it was on the tip of my tongue to beg him *never* to buy a cowboy hat, if he truly loved us.)

"So, my parents do line dancing?" Billy smirked. "My dad too?"

Scary, isn't it? That a boy can live in the same house as his folks and not have a clue what they do with their lives. Scary, but typical, if you ask me.

"Well, yes – didn't you know?" Dad had replied.

Billy shook his head.

"But your father couldn't come to this workshop at the hotel today," Dad had continued, "because of his bad back."

Billy looked confused.

"From hurting it at work?" Dad prompted him.

Billy had looked just as confused.

Not a clue about important details. Not one, tiny clue...

And Billy didn't have much of a clue about learning to shut up, either, as I realized now, sitting in the kids' playground this Sunday evening.

"Still, Ally, if your mum ever comes home, at least she won't find out that your dad's shacked up with someone new!" he said, tactlessly.

Sandie took a sharp intake of breath, knowing that wasn't an entirely sensitive thing to say. But that's Billy for you.

I saw Kyra pause on her swing and narrow her

eyes at me, knowing that there was more of a story to my family than I'd ever let on. But she didn't push me this once, mainly because she's got more of a story too.

And I did find out her story, eventually ... only I won't tell you now. I can't concentrate any more on my writing, 'cause Dad's playing some dreadful country and western track really loud downstairs and Rolf and Winslet are howling along like out-of-tune walruses.

Before I go downstairs and tell Dad that I'm going to report him to the social services for extreme mental cruelty to his children (there's no other way to describe that music), what I *will* say is that Billy was kind of right: I am glad that if Mum happened to wander through the door, all smiles and suntan and outstretched arms, the only romance she'd be hearing about is Grandma and Stanley's (going very well, apparently).

And I'd also like to say that while I love Billy like a brother, I'm so, *so* glad that he isn't going to be one to me.

That would have been *very* weird indeed...

So, until next time, I'll leave you with my top tips for avoiding embarrassing situations:

1) ALWAYS keep spare tampons safely stored in

a zipped-up purse – they have a life of their own and tend to escape from bags when you least expect them to;

2) AVOID any home-made "cocktails" at parties, unless you enjoy being violently sick; and

3) Never EVER tell anyone that your dad does line dancing...

ALLY'S WORLD

PHOTO ALBUM OFFER!
Keep a photographic record of your world!

Just like Ally, there must be loads of things about your own world that you'd like to remember. Here's a great way to keep a reminder of your friends and family, home and pets close at hand in your very own Ally's World photo album.

All you have to do is collect the tokens from the back of Ally's World books 1, 2 and 3 and send them to the address below. To receive the photo album, you must send in one each of Token 1, Token 2 and Token 3.

Remember to include your name and address!

Ally's World Offer
Scholastic Children's Books
Publicity Department
6th Floor
Commonwealth House
1-19 New Oxford Street
London
WC1A 1NU

Token

ALLY'S 2 WORLD